Praise for Philip Reeve

"Philip Reeve is a hugely talented and versatile author...
the emotional journeys of his characters are enthralling,
never sentimental and always believable"
Daily Telegraph

"An absolutely must-read author"
School Librarian

"Philip Reeve's intricate imagination makes
J. K. Rowling feel like Enid Blyton"
Independent

"When I first read Mortal Engines, *I felt as if the*
pages themselves were charged with electricity"
Frank Cottrell Boyce, Guardian

"He conveys big truths while being witty
and playful, and the vocabulary is rich"
Nicolette Jones, Sunday Times

"Witty and thrilling, serious and sensitive, the Mortal Engines
quartet is one of the most daring and imaginative science
fiction adventures ever written for young readers."
Books for Keeps

"The idea behind Philip Reeve's Mortal Engines *books*
has other authors crying 'I wish I'd thought of that!'"
Geraldine McCaughrean, Daily Telegraph

PHILIP REEVE was born in Brighton in 1966. He worked in a bookshop for many years before breaking out and becoming an illustrator – providing cartoons for various books, including several of the *Horrible Histories* series. He has been writing since he was five, but *Mortal Engines* was his first published book. He lives with his wife and son on Dartmoor.

WINNER

CILIP Carnegie Medal
Blue Peter Book of the Year
Nestlé Book Prize, Gold Award
Guardian Children's Fiction Prize

SHORTLISTED

Whitbread Children's Book of the Year
WHSmith People's Choice Awards

No Such Thing As Dragons

with illustrations by the author
PHILIP REEVE

SCHOLASTIC

First published in the UK by Scholastic Children's Books

An imprint of Scholastic Ltd
Euston House, 24 Eversholt Street
London, NW1 1DB, UK
Registered office: Westfield Road, Southam, Warwickshire, CV47 0RA
SCHOLASTIC and associated logos are trademarks and/or
registered trademarks of Scholastic Inc.

ISBN 9781407114835

Printed by Bookmarque Ltd, Croydon, Surrey
Papers used by Scholastic Children's Books are made
from wood grown in sustainable forests.

1 3 5 7 9 10 8 6 4 2

www.scholastic.co.uk/zone

For my mother and father,
Jean and Michael Reeve

1

So they went north, the man and the boy, and the roads narrowed, and big slate-headed mountains reared up ready to eat the sky.

The boy came from a softer country. He didn't like those hills. The hills he was used to were grassy, rounded things like green pillows, with houses on them sometimes, or sheep, and maybe a river at the bottom like a curve of mirror glass. These northern hills were so high he had to lean backwards to try and see the tops of them. They were so rocky that his eyes kept snagging on crags and spears and spines of stone as he looked up and up in search of a summit, in search of an end to the hard confusion of them. Fields of snow showed white up there, spread like raggedy bed sheets across the gaps between black crags. The rivers were white too, spraying in skinny cataracts down the faces of terrifying cliffs. It was as if God had seized hold of this piece of the world in a rage and wrenched it up on end.

The boy's name was Ansel, the man's was Brock. In the lands they'd ridden from, it was already spring. They had seen spring's tokens there: new leaves on the trees and kingcups in the water meadows and sunlight flashing on millstreams and maypoles. But up in these mountains the winter lingered. There was snow on the steep slopes and sleet on the wind. It seemed to Ansel a bad time to be travelling in such country, but Brock had told him that this was the best season by far for the hunting of dragons.

Sometimes as they rode Brock sang old songs, and sometimes he talked. Jokes, stories, comments about the places they were passing. He seemed carefree for a man setting off to fight dragons. Most of the time he didn't even bother to look back at the boy struggling along behind him on his weary pony. He just tossed words over his shoulder and expected Ansel to catch them.

Ansel didn't say anything in reply. He couldn't. "Cat got your tongue?" people asked him sometimes, but he had a tongue all right. It was just words he lacked.

When Ansel was seven years old he suffered two losses. First his mother passed away; then God took the power of speech from him. Before that he had talked as much as any other boy, and sung, too: always singing as he went about his chores, was Ansel. His father had thought there'd be money to be made from a voice like that. When Ansel fell silent his father had said he was just doing it from spite, to rob his family of the fortunes he could have earned by singing. He kicked Ansel, but Ansel wouldn't yelp. He whipped Ansel, but Ansel still wouldn't break his silence. After that, grumpily, he lost interest in the boy. Maybe it was God's doing, after all. He took himself a new wife, and soon there were new children to make plans for.

Ansel's father was a tavern keeper, but you'd have thought him a farmer, the way he reared his children up like livestock, fattening the girls to sell off to the sons of rich merchants in town, the boys to farm out as apprentices and servants to wealthy men.

When Johannes Brock stopped at the humpbacked inn to water his horse and his pack pony and happened to mention that he was looking for a boy to serve him on a journey he had to make into the north, Ansel's father grinned and rubbed his big red hands together. He chivvied his sons into line like bullocks at market. "This one here's Ludovico, master; small for his age, but tough. Or what about Martin here? He'll serve you well; you'll serve the gentleman well, Martin, won't you?" He passed over Ansel without bothering to mention him. When Brock asked about the boy, he only shrugged and said, "Ansel's afflicted. Mute."

But it turned out that Johannes Brock was tickled by the prospect of a silent servant. "He cannot read or write, I suppose?"

"Oh no, sir!"

"Then a man's secrets would be safe with such a servant. And no chattering, either. I cannot abide chattering." He walked all round Ansel. He looked like a man with secrets: tall and dark-eyed, with his copper-coloured hair curling round his handsome face, and a thin pale scar like a snail's trail winding down one cheek and into the fair stubble on his jaw. His clothes were travel-stained but rich, the tunic with its pierced patterns of diamond and teardrop-shaped holes, the thick woollen travelling cloak. He smelled of horses and metal and far-off wars. If St Michael himself (thought Ansel) were to come down from Heaven to walk upon the earth, then he would take a shape like that.

Once Ansel's father saw that the stranger was interested, he started to remember Ansel's good points. "My Ansel's an obedient boy, sir. Ten years old. Strong and healthy. Bright, despite his affliction. His mother's favourite, he was, God rest her soul. Of course, it would break my poor old heart, sir, if I had to part with him. Unless the price was right. . ."

He was wasting his breath. Brock had already decided. A purse of money was passed over. In less time than it would have taken him to pour the stranger a flagon of beer, Ansel's father had gold in his pocket and one less mouth to feed. It made him affectionate as he bundled Ansel's spare clothes in a bag and packed him off with the traveller. "You take care of him, sir!" he called, puffing alongside as they set out, with Ansel on the pony. "You send him safe home when your journey's done. Where is it that you are bound for anyway, if you'll pardon me for asking, my lord?"

"To the north country." Brock grinned down at him from the heights of his horse. "I am bound for the north, to hunt dragons."

2

It had sounded like a joke, back there in the lowlands, where spring was already prising open the pretty pink blossom in the orchards. There were no such things as dragons, were there? Only in stories. Only in tales told round the hearth on winter's nights, to set you shivering with cosy fear. Only in pictures.

Riding north with Brock, Ansel remembered the painting of St George he'd seen in the big church in town. The saint had been all in armour, but bareheaded, with a golden halo balanced jauntily on his curls. The poor princess he'd come to save had a wide white forehead and yellow hair, and she looked surprisingly calm for someone who'd been sent out into the wilds as dragon food. She wore cloth-of-gold, and she carried a bunch of tall white lilies, perhaps as a sort of garnish. As for the dragon itself, Ansel recalled that it had looked like a bald green chicken with a lizard's head and the wings of a bat. Its wide-open mouth was vermilion red, and so was the blood that uncurled like red fern fronds from its breast as it leaned helpfully on to the point of the saint's lance.

He wondered if St George had had a boy to serve him, and if so, why the boy had not been in the picture. Was it that he was just not important enough? Or was it, perhaps, that he was in the beast's belly?

Still, it was hard to believe in dragons, hard to *really* believe in them during the first few days of the journey, as they rode in spring sunshine up the white, dusty road which rose almost imperceptibly through higher and higher hills towards the cloud-shrouded peaks ahead. Brock went in front, while Ansel booted the sleepy pony along in his wake.

The oil-cloth bundles that held Brock's armour bounced on the pony's flanks, sounding like sacks of kitchen pans.

Brock didn't speak much at first, except to say, "Fetch this", or "Bring that", or "Look to the horses" – much the same things that Ansel was used to hearing from his father and his brothers. But Brock managed to say it with that grin of his, which made Ansel eager to please him. Sometimes, when he did his duties well, the tall man would reward him with a pat on the head, and on one memorable day a slab of apple cake from a stall in a town they passed through. He tried pretending that Johannes Brock was his father as they rode along. It made him feel proud to see the way people's eyes followed the big man when they rode through towns and villages. Although he was still a little scared of him, he thought it would be better to have Brock as a father than his own. He couldn't imagine Brock selling off *his* sons for purses of gold.

Each evening, when they rode into some small town and found an inn to stop at, Brock's manner underwent a subtle change. He would sit taller on his horse, and pull back the scrag of blanket to bare the hilt of the big sword which hung from his saddle. When anyone at the inn asked him his name he said, "I am Johannes Von Brock. I hunt dragons."

In those lands, far to the north of Ansel's home, people took talk of dragons seriously. No one had actually *seen* one, but everyone was eager to hear from someone who had. Fellow travellers invited Brock to dine with them so that he could tell them the stories of his adventures and all the dragons he had stalked and killed. "Worms" he called them, as if they were no more fearful to him than the pink earthworms that Ansel used to play with in his mother's vegetable patch when he was small. Brock seemed modest, but he had a way of talking that could silence a whole tavern. "I've hunted these beasts all over Christendom. Faced my first when I was not much older than my squire here. Transcarpathia, Haute-Savoy, the Hartzberg: now here. It's my calling, you could say. Every time I slay a worm I vow that one's the last, and I settle down with what I've earned. Yet every time the old itch returns to me and I find myself back on the road, trailing another damned worm. Still, I'd have no other life. It beats soldiering, or seafaring, or *working* for a living. . ."

The men among his audience always wanted to

know how he tracked the beasts, where they made their lairs and how they fought. Brock answered their questions patiently while the women gazed at the silvery scar on his beautiful face as if they were longing to kiss him better. Sometimes he opened the top of his tunic and pulled his shirt aside to show his listeners the curved ivory fang, as long as a man's forefinger, which hung on a thong around his neck. Then the women sighed, wide-eyed and wistful at the thought of the dangers the young knight had lived through. Brock basked in their adoration like a cat on a sunny sill.

And Ansel? Ansel made sure that the horses were safe in their stables. He liked the horses. Brock's big mare, Snow, and the stocky pony called Brezel who carried Ansel and the food and cookpot and the spare cloaks and clothes and Brock's armour. They were so big and powerful, with all those muscles and tendons sliding under their skin and those gaping, snorting nostrils. They were almost like dragons themselves, he thought (at least he did until the night he sneaked a look in Brock's saddlebag and caught a glimpse of what *real* dragons looked like). He groomed them and fed them, and he polished the saddles and girths and stirrup leathers and his master's tall travelling boots, while the children of the place and the rougher men tried to make him speak, regarding his muteness as a challenge. "The dragon's waiting!" they would tell him, pointing at the mountains which walled off the northern sky. "Big as a house, hot as an oven, huffing out flames and cinders and hungry for Christian flesh. What do you say to that, boy? Eh?" Then they would make munching sounds, and laugh.

And Ansel laughed with them in his soundless way, but he never really thought it was funny.

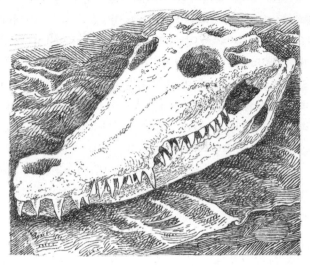

3

By then the road was climbing steeply, winding up and up along the course of a river which grew narrower, fiercer and louder with each day. The air smelled of the sap of pine trees which stood in dark congregations on the hillsides. The sky ahead was full of mountains, and the mountains were bigger than any mountain that Ansel had ever seen, even in his dreams.

"See that high one there in the middle, wrapped

up in cloud?" asked Brock one morning, pointing to it and half turning in his saddle to make sure that Ansel was looking in the right place. "That's where we're going. The reports I've heard all agree that it's haunted by a monstrous worm. The peasants live in terror of it. The landgrave who rules over them will pay me well if I can rid him of it."

An inn stood at the roadside in the lee of wooded crags. It had a fresh green bush hung above the door by way of a sign, and its landlady was a widow woman, youngish and red-cheeked, with a fat plait of fair hair coiled round her head like the rim on a pie crust. She enjoyed Brock's dragon stories so much that she took him to her own room that night so he could tell her more. Ansel, for the first time in his life, slept all alone, curled up on the floor beside the dragon hunter's empty bed.

Except that he could not sleep. The wind hissed in the pines behind the inn. It came in through gaps in the shutters and rummaged among the rushes on the floor. Mice scuffled in the thatch. The dragons which he found it so hard to believe in when the sun was shining seemed much more plausible as he lay there alone in the darkness. He imagined them out there in the silence of the mountains, soaring over those pitiless summits on their leathern wings. He imagined burps of flame from their long jaws lighting up the cols and corries, splaying their bat-black shadows on the cliffs. Maybe one was above him now, wheeling above the inn, looking down with its cold black eyes. From up there the thatched roof would be a pale, shag-edged square on the midnight land, like a patch stitched on a blanket. . .

He said aloud, "There's no such thing as dragons," and shifted himself closer to where Brock's sword and saddlebags lay in the corner, hoping that they would give him some comfort. He lay with eyes open, looking at the shapes of the bags. They were leather bags, made hide-side out with the hair left on. In the dark room they looked like furry, sleeping dogs. The rest of their baggage was stored in the stable, but Brock trusted no one but Ansel with those bags. The larger one held Brock's spare clothes and shaving gear and other things a gentleman carried with him on the road. As for the smaller, Ansel had been told that he wasn't to look inside it.

He was an obedient boy by nature, and it had never occurred to him before to even wonder what his master kept in that bag. Now, alone, he started to think, *What would it matter if I took a peek?* Was it treasure that his master was carrying? Some charm for the slaying of dragons? Or a souvenir of past victories?

The inn creaked. The trees sighed. The voices of Brock and the widow woman came indistinctly through the stone wall from a neighbouring room. Ansel threw off the cloak he had covered himself with and went quietly to the bags. He carried the smaller of them to a place where a big shard of moonlight came through a crack in the window shutter. He did not open it straight away but felt it, trying to read with his fingers the long shape which lay inside. A rounded softness with a hard heart, like a swaddled stone, but too light to be a stone. He drew a deep breath and unknotted the cords that tied the bag shut. The swathed shape was the only thing inside. He lifted it out. It was shaped like a giant's spoon.

He was very afraid lest Brock should come into the room and find him crouched there by the open bag, but it was too late now to turn back; he had to know what the thing was. Quickly, like someone eagerly unwrapping a parcel, he tore off the cloth that it was wrapped in.

It was a skull as long as Ansel's arm. A wedge of pitted bone that tapered to a thin knob of a snout. There was no doubting what manner of beast it had belonged to. The snout pointed jauntily upwards, as if it were still sniffing the air for prey, still hungry for boy-flesh, even in this bony, bodiless state. The wicked eyeholes were set high up on top, in front of the scalloped hooks and hinges which worked the jaw. The rest of it was all mouth: a self-satisfied zigzagging smirk stitched with white daggers. It had teeth enough for a dozen dragons.

Ansel stared at it a long time, but it didn't get any less frightening. He closed it back in its coverings and replaced the bag in its corner and slid back under his cloak. He was shivering slightly, and every time the old inn creaked or shifted he pictured a dragon settling on the roof. But after a while he must have slept, because when he woke a bell was clanging somewhere and he could see sunlight through that gap in the shutter and Brock was prodding him awake with the toe of his boot and telling him to go and attend to the saddling of the horses.

4

A few hours after they left the inn, the road dipped
sharply into a fold of the land, sloping down so
steep that they had to dismount and lead the horses.
Brock grumbled, angry to be throwing away all the
height they'd gained. But Ansel was relieved. He
welcomed anything that would delay their coming
to that terrible mountain which waited for them
ahead, swathed in clouds and dragon-haunted.
Every time he shut his eyes he saw again the long

skull in his master's saddlebag. All night his dreams had been filled with flying dragons. Hot coals had rained from their jaws and the smoke of their breath had darkened the sky. Their ivory teeth were so sharp and fierce that he doubted even Brock's great sword could wipe those grins off their scaly faces.

The bottom of that cleave was filled with trees – good, full-sized beech and birch, with a river twining between them. There was a whisper of spring in the sheltered air. Not much, only the faintest blush of fresh green in the beech-tops and the quick singing of a few birds, but welcome after the harshness of the heights.

When they reached the valley floor, Brock flung himself full-length on a patch of grass. "Dear Christ, I'm weary of this travelling! Ansel, bring the wine and the bread. We'll rest here a while."

He rested, gnawing on one of the small loaves which the affectionate widow lady at the inn had given them. Meanwhile, Ansel went down towards the river. He was looking for a place where Brezel and Snow could drink. The floor of the woods was all boulders, with pools of clear water between them. The river was the colour of metal, swirling between bare trees. Beyond those trees there was no sky, just the steep flank of a hill rising almost sheer, reminding him of the bleak heights that he was headed for. Not wanting to look at it, Ansel looked down instead.

That was when he saw it. A shape flashed across the pool at his feet: the reflection of something with big, spread wings swooping low over the trees above his head.

He pelted back to where he'd left Brock and the horses, trying clumsily to cross himself as he ran, plunging into the pools, scraping himself on low branches. He burst out into the thin sunlight pointing upwards, desperate to warn his master that the dragon was upon them. It must have sensed by some magic that the hunter was on his way, and flown down from its lonely mountain to meet him on the road.

"What is it, boy? What—?" Brock was scrambling up, looking alarmed. The horses, untroubled, cropped the grass a little way off. Brock shielded his eyes, scanning the sky. Ansel wondered why he didn't run to fetch his sword. Instead, he started to laugh.

"You thought it was the worm!" He threw back his head. "Christ, you believed it!"

Confused, Ansel looked up at the sky. Far up the valley the big grey wings flapped steadily in sunlight, carrying the heron away towards quieter fishing grounds.

Only a heron. . . Ansel tried to laugh at himself, but the fear was still in him and the best he could manage was a crooked smile.

Brock looked at him, and stopped laughing, seeing the real fear in the boy's face. He came closer, and patted Ansel's shoulder. "Ansel," he said, "I'll tell you my secret. My secret's safe with you, isn't it?"

Ansel nodded. Brock stooped down so that his face was on a level with the boy's. He said slowly and clearly, "There are no such things as dragons."

Ansel watched him, puzzled. Was this a joke? A test? What?

"I've been halfway across the world," said Brock. "I went a-soldiering when I was young, and I saw eagles and tigers and whale-fish and saracens, but I've never seen a dragon yet, nor heard of one that was anything more than a story. They don't exist, Ansel. If they did, we'd all have seen them. Kings and dukes would keep them in their menageries. Rich men would wear dragon-skin hats and dragon-scale shoes, and serve roast dragon at their banquets. But they don't. And why? Because there's no such animal, that's why. Maybe there was once, but Noah never found room for them on his ark – it would be a hazard on a boat, I'd reckon, a beast that belches fire. And even if they had survived, you don't really think we'd find one up here in all this snow and wind, do you? A dragon's supposed to be a huge lizard, isn't it? Lizards bake themselves on summer rocks; hide up and sleep when the weather turns chill. How would one keep itself warm up on those white heights? With its own fiery breath?"

Ansel opened his mouth to protest, so surprised that he had forgotten he was dumb. He pointed questioningly at the dragon's tooth which dangled on its thong round Brock's neck. Brock looked down, touched it. "This?"

Ansel nodded. Wasn't that proof of dragons?

"I bought this in Aleppo. A tiger's tooth, the man who sold it told me. As for this scar, I got it when I was young; I pulled my little sister's pigtails and she pushed me down the stairs. I cut my face open on a doornail."

Ansel didn't want to believe him. Surely not *all* of Brock's bravery could be lies. What about the skull? He forgot that he was not meant to have seen it and pointed questioningly to the bag on Snow's saddle.

Brock laughed again. "So you've been prying, have you? I might have known that telling a boy *not* to look in a bag is the surest way to make him do so. . ." He strode to where the mare was grazing and opened the bag, tugging the thing out carelessly, uncovering its huge and hungry grin. Ansel did his best to look brave, but he could not help flinching. The thing looked so evil, and so pleased with itself.

"I picked this up from a trader in Venice," said Brock. "It comes from Africa. It's the head bone of a monster called a corkindrille, which is a big breed of newt that swims in the waters of the river Nile and eats up little blackamoors for breakfast. It's the nearest thing to a living, breathing dragon that I ever heard tell of. But it *isn't* a dragon. It's got no wings, no fiery breath, no voice, no magic stone in its head. It's just a big animal. Isn't that right?" he asked the skull, and worked its jaws so that it seemed to answer him, "*That's right, Brock!*"

He wrapped the skull again and stuffed it in his bag. When he came back to where Ansel waited he was still chuckling. "You look as shocked as a wrung-necked goose," he said. "You're probably wondering what we're making this hard journey for, then, if there's no worm to slaughter at the end of it?"

23

Ansel nodded.

"Well, that's the *real* secret. You see, just because worms are only stories doesn't mean that half of mankind aren't fool enough to believe in them."

He took Ansel by the shoulders and turned him bodily to face the looming cliffs and buttresses of the mountains ahead. He said, "In places like this, where the winters are hard and the peasants are stupid, no one doubts but there are dragons on the heights. Every time a sheep is killed or a goatherd goes missing, the old stories that their grandmothers scared them with bubble up anew in their heads, till they can think of nothing but the worm. When we ride in promising to deliver them from the terror, they'll welcome us as heroes.

"So we'll go up into their high pastures, you and I. There'll be no one up there this early in the year, and there's bound to be a shepherd's hut or a handy cave where we can shelter for a night or two. Just long enough for word to get round, and folk to start wondering whether we'll ever come back. And then, like Our Lord, we'll rise on the third day. We'll come back down carrying friend corkindrille's skull bone on a stick, and telling the people what a hard fight we had before their worm was slain. Of course I'll have to dress the old skull up a bit; some meat and brains from a dead sheep to make it look fresher than it is. No one will know it's not the head of a dragon. Then there'll be feasting, grateful women, maybe a few small gifts, all graciously accepted. And all I need do to get it is lie up a while in a shepherd's hut. Better than hunting dragons, isn't it?"

Ansel nodded. In truth, he wasn't sure how he felt. He knew he should be glad that he needn't fear the dragon any more, but somehow he felt that Brock had taken something from him. It had all been lies.

They rode on and quickly came in sight of that great grim mountain again. Cloud shadows swooped over the crinkled lower slopes; the heights were chained with glaciers and tangled in ropes of mist. Ansel was still afraid of it, but now what scared him was mostly the thought of so much height, such cold. Its terrors had become everyday terrors. It no longer held anything as marvellous or horrifying as a dragon.

5

They came near that day's end to a town that was trying to be a city. There had been thin, wintry rain all afternoon, but by that hour the evening breeze was herding the clouds away and the westering sun showed through, lighting the town's tall walls so that the stones shone like scales. The town lay in a hollow of the mountains with a long lake below it and a white road winding up to its gates and the hard sheer shoulders of the mountains going up steep and sudden behind it, rising towards that one cloud-capped peak that overtopped all the rest. Afterwards Ansel would never be able to remember what the town's name was, but he would remember for the rest of his life the name of the mountain. It was called the Drachenberg.

"That's where we're bound, boy," said Brock, with his narrowed eyes on the mountain. "But we'll stop here for the night. One last night in a comfortable bed, before our climb begins."

At the town gate a fire burned smokily in a metal basket and guards with halberds stepped forward to bar the travellers' way. "You're Johannes Von Brock, the dragon hunter?" asked their leader.

Brock swept his cap off. "You have heard of me, it seems."

"The whole country's heard of your coming," said the guard, his eyes going up and down Brock, peering at every detail. "The landgrave wants to see you. Told us to bring you to his palace."

Brock sat straighter in his saddle. "Lead on," he said.

The guard captain and two of his men shouldered their halberds and led the way, through the gate and up deep, narrow, cobbled streets. In the heart of the town, towering high over the thatch of houses and the long, planked lofts of the wool mills a big new church was rising. The fresh stone of the half-finished spire was bone-coloured, pale against the darkness of the mountain. Masons were still at work up there when Brock and Ansel rode by. Their giddy gantries swayed in the wind, and the pecking sounds of their hammers and chisels fell thinly like the calls of stonechats into the open space between the church and the houses which hemmed it round. Fresh stores of stone lay heaped under flapping canvas, waiting their turn to be hoisted aloft and carved into stone prayers.

Behind the church was a low grey house they called the Palace. It was shut tight, unwelcoming. A carved stone shield above the doors bore the arms of the family who ruled the place: a winged dragon with a pointed tongue. Snow lay in heaps against the walls. It took a lot of knocking with the butt of the guard captain's halberd before the huge doors grumbled open. Servants peered at Brock. Inside, the sounds of the town were so muffled by the thick walls that Ansel felt as if someone had stuffed lint into his ears. A priest's bare shanks flashed under the hem of his habit as he came running to lead the travellers to his master.

The landgrave awaited them in a panelled room,

in front of a deep fireplace where a peat fire burned, not giving out much heat. On the cowl of the fireplace the dragon emblem of his family spread its wings again. He turned as the visitors entered. He was not an old man, but he had the wary, careworn face of a shaved sheep. It must have been a tiring business being lord of such a cold and backward place. He looked exhausted. His eyes were the colour of mussel shells. He had gnawed the sides of his thumbs ragged, and his long fingers never stopped moving, telling over the beads of the rosary that hung from his belt. On a table beside him his servants were laying out bread and cheeses and cold meat and wine. Ansel ate hungrily while his master and the landgrave talked.

"What brings you to our town, stranger?" asked the landgrave, in a tired-out voice. "There are rumours about you among the common people. They say that you kill dragons."

Brock nodded graciously. "I am Johannes Von Brock, landgrave. This boy is my squire. It was good of you to meet me; I should have asked to see you in any case, for I'm told you have need of my skills. Your people are right. I am a hunter of dragons."

For the first time the landgrave stopped looking weary and grew interested.

"I have heard that this region is ravaged by a most troublesome worm, and I have come to rid you of it," said Brock. "This is the best season for worm-hunting. There is still snow and ice on the heights, and it drives the creatures down on to the lower slopes for food. That means I have a chance of meeting them without making the impossible climb to their eyries."

The landgrave nibbled the corners of his thumbs. "This district has always been dragon-haunted," he said, and he shivered a little inside his expensive robes. "There have long been stories told of a beast upon the mountain. The Dragon's Hill, it's called. The peasants up there are weak and superstitious. The pass through the mountains was closed by a rock fall many years ago and they will not clear it because they are afraid of the dragon. There is said to be copper and even silver in the mountain, but my miners will not go up there to mine it; they hear the peasants talking of their dragon, and they too grow fearful. This could be a rich town, if it were not for that dragon. But you and I are educated men, Brock. We know that there are no such things as dragons, don't we?"

Ansel stopped eating and looked at the

landgrave. He wondered if the man had seen through Brock's ruse and was about to expose him as a charlatan. What would happen to Brock then? And what would happen to his boy?

Brock looked watchful for a moment, too. Then he recovered himself and nodded, as if he had often heard the same complaint from other educated men in other places. He said, "There is the dragon, my lord, and then there is the *fear* of the dragon. It is hard to say which is worse. And even if you doubt the dragon, you must admit the fear is real."

The landgrave smiled distantly and turned to the window, which stood open to let out the thick smoke from the fire. A rusty-coloured sunset was staining the sky behind the half-finished spire of the new church. He said, "I told them that once we had our cathedral then the creature would be driven away. But they only grow more credulous and more afraid. They swear that they have heard the dragon shrieking on the heights. Even here in the town its voice has been heard. They say that it devoured a shepherd last year, up on the summer pastures.

"In the old times, before they heard the word of Christ, the people used to tether a girl on the mountain each springtime as an offering to the serpent. That's been stopped now. But who knows? Most of the villages up there are too small to have their own church, their own priest to guide them. Who knows what sins their fear might drive them to?"

"Then let me kill it," said Brock, pouring more wine for himself.

"Kill what? The dragon, or the fear of the dragon?"

"Both," replied Brock. He had opened the top of his tunic and the ivory fang shone wickedly in the hollow of his throat. The firelight silvered the old scar on his cheek. He had the look of a man who killed dragons.

The landgrave studied him. Did he believe the dragon was real? Or did he not? Ansel could not tell. But either way, he seemed to think that there would be something to be gained by sending Brock up the mountain. He said, "The peasants tell us that the creature makes its lair high on the Drachenberg, in a cave beside a river of ice, above the village called Knochen. You may stay here tonight, set off in the morning. My secretary will draw a map to show you the way. I fear it will be a hard journey for you."

Brock stretched like a cat. "I'm used to hard journeys," he said. "I've climbed higher mountains. All I ask is your priests' blessing on me and the boy before we set out. Oh, and gold, of course."

"So you must be paid for fighting this evil?" asked the landgrave slyly.

Brock spread his hands. His grin said everything. "How I wish I could do it for nothing but the love of God and the grateful thanks of your peasants, my lord! But this is a sinful world we live in, and a man needs money if he's to make his way in it. Money for horses, fodder, food. Clothes for myself and the boy. Money for harness and weapons. That sword of mine's no kitchen knife. It's Spanish steel, the only kind that will bite through dragon hide. It costs money, a blade like that. It will cost me money to have a good smith repair it when I've scuffed and blunted it on your dragon's scales."

The landgrave let out a wan laugh. "But dragons keep hoards, don't they? Greedy creatures, so the stories say. Don't they sleep in caves filled with gold and diamonds and rubies? Can't you simply help yourself to a share of our dragon's treasure when you've slain him, master Brock?"

Brock did not laugh. "You don't know these worms like I do, my lord. You only know old stories of them. I've hunted the fell creatures in half the hills of Christendom, and I've never yet seen more in their lairs than heaps of dead men's bones. If you want me to kill your dragon, you'll have to pay me."

The landgrave nodded to one of his waiting servants, and the man took something from a wooden casket and brought it to Brock. It was an ornate crucifix made from white gold, buttery-coloured in the firelight, not big, but heavy. Brock took it, weighing it in the palm of his hand.

"It is one of the treasures of my family," said the landgrave. "I would not part with it unless the need was very great. But it will be yours if you can rid us of the dragon – and the fear of the dragon."

The meeting left Brock in a bad mood. Ansel had never seen him angry before. He turned pale, and two spots of colour burned high on his cheeks. "That upstart!" he muttered. "Landgrave of nothing, yet he treats me like a mountebank. You heard the way he spoke, Ansel? As good as called me a liar."

But you are *a liar*, Ansel thought, and though he couldn't say it, Brock seemed to hear. He looked at Ansel and his temper passed. He laughed.

"Well, you're right. But I have my pride, you know. It's one thing to live by playing on the fears of fools, and another to have someone remind you of it. A little respect, that's all I ask. But the world's changing, Ansel. Even in outlandish places like this we meet with educated men. Soon there will be so many of them that no one will take seriously talk of dragons any more. And what will I do for a profession then?"

Ansel would have liked to stay in the warm, but he had the horses to tend to before the light died. "You can't trust his reverence's servants to care for them," said Brock, sending him back out into the frosty dusk. "Townsmen. What do they know of horses? Go and see they're properly stabled while there's still light."

Brock was right, just as he always was. The landgrave's servants had tethered the horses in an old shippen, and filled a manger with hay, but the sweat of the journey still lay on the animals' flanks, and they were ragged and muddy from their day on the wet roads. Ansel crooned soft noises to them while he rubbed them down with a knot of frayed rope. He picked stubborn clags of mud from their bellies. Carefully he combed them, undoing the elf-knots in their tails and forelocks. They stood calmly, breath a-smoulder in the cold air, leaning some of their weight against him while he knelt down to tug off the burrs which had snagged on their fetlocks like spiny, biscuit-coloured stars. He gripped their nobbly ankles and they patiently lifted up their feet for him so that he could scrape the packed rinds of mud and road stones from the hollows of their hoofs.

Coming out of the shippen, closing the hurdle carefully behind him and latching it shut, he turned to see the last light of the day shining on the spire of the new church. Gargoyles leaned leering from the tower's sides, all with forked tongues and lizard faces and bat wings, as if thoughts of the dragon had kept creeping into the heads of the stone cutters while they were carving them. It must be like that, thought Ansel, to live in dragon country. Whatever the time of day, whatever the time of year, you would be thinking always of the dragon. It would be there constantly, just under the edges of your other thoughts. It would get into your dreams.

Behind the church the mountain hunched huge and bruise-black into the clouds. Not hard to see how it came by its name. Those five sharp peaks were like the horns and spines of a sleeping dragon;

those long walls of cliff and scree were its flanks and its folded wings. The Dragon's Hill.

And as he stood there looking at it a sound reached him, blown on the wind. A yowling, caterwauling cry, echoing off icy rocks and the floors of frozen corries. Ansel felt his heart stop and start again. The noise caught him by his throat and pushed him back against the shippen wall. A man passing on his way to the landgrave's kitchens stopped and looked towards the mountain and quickly crossed himself. "Lord God defend us from the dragon," Ansel heard him say.

6

They stayed in the landgrave's guest quarters that night and went on at dawn, damp with holy water, the windblown blessings of the town's priests echoing in their ears. Word of the dragon hunter's arrival had spread swiftly, and despite the cold a crowd gathered to see them out of town. For a while a band of excited children and a good few grown-ups too ran after the riders, shouting questions and warnings about the beast on the mountain, and laying wagers among themselves about what Brock's chances were. But they did not stray far beyond the town walls.

Soon Ansel and his master were riding alone up a road which wound uncertainly across the steep foothills, forever twisting back upon itself, as if it were having second thoughts about going too near the mountain. Every few miles a crude stone cross marked the way, and other crosses showed on the steep hillsides, made from wood and hammered into the thin turf like fence posts in an effort to nail some goodness to this hard, cold country. The woods of beech and birch gave way to black stands of pine, with sometimes a cleared meadow between them. Then even the pines thinned out, till there were just a few, standing like tattered standards between the crags. Jackdaws slid past on the breeze, watching the travellers with their icy blue eyes. Their cries clanged off the rocks. At last, in the hour before dusk, the road heaved itself over a stone ridge as sharp as a dragon's spine, and let them down into a valley where buildings clumped at the edge of a tarn.

The village was no more than a huddle of huts. Thatch was heaped above their log walls in hopeless mounds, giving them the look of cowpats that had fallen from a great height. If Ansel hadn't known better, he might have thought they were dragon spoor. Around them women were working, white headdresses bobbing like gulls as they turned to watch the riders. On strips of near-vertical field, men were at work with picks and mattocks, clearing rocks, or maybe gathering more to add to the wavering stone walls which reached up the slopes behind the village. A clumsy fishing boat bobbed on the tarn, batted this way and that by the cats' paws which chased across the water.

"This is the place," said Brock, urging Snow downhill towards the village as a gaggle of children started up to meet him. Then, seeing the shabby figure who came with them, "Oh, God's bones! What's *he* doing here?"

The man was a mendicant friar, a travelling holy man who went from place to place, praising God and living on whatever he could beg from the villagers who welcomed him. You would think pickings would be thin in that starved mountain country, but the friar looked healthy enough: a stocky, cheerful man with bat ears and a scrubby tonsure. Raspberry-red boots pierced with patterns of little holes flashed beneath his dowdy habit. He held up his arms when he recognized Brock, shouting, "God be thanked! Our prayers are answered! A soldier of Christ is come to deliver us all from this evil serpent!"

The village children gaped saucer-eyed at the newcomers. Some took the friar's hint and fell on their faces by the road, thanking God in reedy voices.

"Don't you know who this is?" the friar called, turning to shout over the children's heads at the men and women of the place, who were leaving off their work and coming to greet the riders. "This is Johannes Von Brock, the famous dragon killer! God has granted him the strength to keep good Christians safe from creatures of Satan like the one that haunts your mountain! Make him welcome! The Lord has heard our prayers!"

The villagers clustered around the horses, reaching out to touch Brock's boots, and even Ansel's, as if they thought some of the dragon hunter's luck and virtue might have rubbed off on his boy. Wary, weathered faces split into smiles. Village maidens blushed and dimpled. Pointing fingers jabbed towards the mountain, and a dozen eager voices started telling Brock of places where the dragon had been seen.

"Enough! Enough!" Brock held up his hand to

quiet them. His eyes flicked back and forth across their hopeful faces, lingering on those of the prettier girls and women. "My squire and I will sleep here tonight, and tomorrow we'll ride out to settle your dragon. But our road has been hard. Later I'll be glad to hear whatever you can tell me of the beast. But first I need a place to rest, stabling for my horses. And a word with Father Flegel," he added, with a stern glance at the friar.

The head man's house was quiet once the family who lived there had been hustled out to allow the dragon hunter some privacy. Quiet, at least, if you didn't count the odd fart from the cows who shared it, or the constant subdued mumblings of the entire population of Knochen, who had gathered round outside to see what happened next.

Ansel went to fetch water, and came back to find Brock deep in hushed, angry talk with the friar. The friar shut up fast when Ansel entered, but Brock flapped a hand, motioning to Ansel to come closer. "The boy does not have the power of speech. You can say what you like. What brings you here, Flegel?"

"*Father* Flegel," said the friar sulkily.

Brock looked down at Ansel, who was pouring

water into a bowl for him to bathe his feet in. "Flegel was a monk until they expelled him for his heretical views and filthy habits," he explained. "Now he shambles from place to place as he pleases, selling indulgences and fraudulent relics. . ."

"The shinbone of St Ursula was not fraudulent!" grumbled Flegel.

"And nor was the little finger of St Martin, I suppose," said Brock, "or St Anthony's jawbone – you've sold three of those, to my sure knowledge. You're a leech, Flegel. You're God's lamprey. The mystery is, what you are doing in this scoured-out country?"

Flegel gathered his robes about him, straining for dignity. "I go where God summons me," he said. "And anyway, I heard that you were travelling in this region. That told me these villages must be full of frightened, superstitious fools. Why, I'll go there and soften them up ready for Brock's coming, I said. He'll be glad of me. And so you should be, Brock. I caught a couple of their sheep on my way; gutted them and left them near the fields, where they were soon found. You should have heard these fools howl, Brock! They're convinced that the dragon did it. It seems a shepherd from this place vanished on the high pastures back last summertime, and it's left them all as jumpy as a bag of frogs."

"You didn't kill the shepherd, I take it?"

"Brock! Don't joke about such things! As if I, a man of Christ, would. . . No. The man was killed by bandits, probably, passing through from one valley to another. Or wolves. There must be a hundred ways to die upon a hill like this without any need to blame a dragon."

Brock nodded. "Have you ever climbed a mountain, Flegel? Right up, I mean, not just scuttling through the passes. It's another world up there. Endless ice, and snow, and terrible rocks, and the cold sharp enough to flay the flesh off you. Storms of wind and snow that can blow in suddenly, in any season. Maybe the poor fool froze, or tumbled down a chasm."

Flegel spread his hands, and grinned. "I know, I know, but try telling that to these peasants. Whenever anything goes awry here, it is always their dragon they blame."

Brock gave his snorting laugh. He pulled his feet out of the cooling water and dried them on the hem of Flegel's robe and said to Ansel, "Go and find that head man. Let him know we're ready now to eat, and hear his stories."

7

White porridge, black broth, grey salt meat. The villagers laid the best food they could before the dragon hunter, and it was as colourless as the mountain they lived on. They hadn't much left at this end of winter. Their flat barley beer left a taste of rust in Ansel's mouth. The head man said, "If we had known of your coming, my lord, we'd have killed a pig."

"Kill it in the morning," said Brock, through a

gristly mouthful of old mutton. "We'll feast when I come back with the dragon's head."

He seemed content, thought Ansel, watching him as he ate and drank. The whole village was watching him, gathered round the small table in the head man's hut. They stood in a ring and watched wide-eyed, mothers pushing their children to the front, as if they'd never seen a man eat before. Between bites, Brock grinned at them encouragingly. He winked at the children, and eyed up the women like a fox in a dovecote. When his plate was empty he pushed the table aside and stretched out his long legs in front of him so that the light of the peat fire danced on his tall shiny boots. "Now, tell me about this beast of yours," he said.

Ansel was shoved aside in the rush as villagers pressed forward to tell the newcomer their own version of the dragon story. There was an eagerness about them that he didn't like. They had a sly way of looking at Brock when Brock wasn't looking at them, as if they had some secret they were keeping to themselves. But maybe he was just imagining it. Brock did not seem to notice, certainly. He sat leaning forward in his seat, his face intent, granting them all his attention as they told him their tales of the dragon.

"It has a face like a cat—"

"Like a stoat—"

"Like an owl—"

"It cries like a buzzard—"

"It took ten cattle last winter from the field up there, behind the village—"

"It ripped the roof off a barn to get at my milch-cow—"

"It ate all the sheep on the summer pastures, and when we went looking for them we found only bones!"

"Father Flegel said that it took a shepherd, too," said Brock.

The villagers nodded. "He had gone high on the mountain. Too high. . ." said one.

If Brock had hoped to goad them into greater terror by reminding them of the lost man, he was disappointed. Talking of it made them seem sober; almost shamed. They shuffled back from him, hanging their heads, looking down at their rag-wrapped feet or slyly sideways at each other's faces.

"This mountain has long been the habitation of dragons," said Flegel dolefully. Ansel guessed the friar was feeling peeved that the villagers' attention had been stolen from him by Brock. He seemed to puff up like a toad when their eyes turned back to him. "Why, Marcus Aurelius himself, the emperor of Rome, when he came riding through these high passes at the head of all his legions, heard tales of great serpents living on the heights. Of all the dragons of all the mountains of the earth, the one that haunts this mountain is the oldest and most wicked."

"Well, it won't be haunting here for much longer," Brock said firmly. "Tomorrow at first light I shall go up into the high places, and find your dragon, and put an end to it. And to ensure my victory, I shall be taking Father Flegel with me."

Ansel saw Flegel turn and stare at Brock, aghast. "Me?" he squeaked. "But I am just a poor friar, I cannot make such a journey; I am infirm and filled with feebleness. The spirit is willing, you understand, but the flesh is weak. . ."

"There's certainly plenty of it," muttered Brock, glancing at the friar's fat belly.

"No," declared Flegel, "I shall stay here. But fear not, for my prayers shall go with you. . ."

"God will help you climb, brother," said Brock, with a playful grin. "How much more powerful will your prayers be if you can hurl them into the very maw of the beast? What am I, after all? Just a soldiering man, with a knack for killing dragons.

But if this particular dragon is as old and evil as you say, I shall need a man of God at my side."

The villagers mumbled their agreement. Ansel felt guilty when he looked at them. Hope was softening each winter-worn face like butter soaking into hot bread. They believed in their dragon, and they believed Brock and Flegel were going to deliver them from it. Their belief was so strong that it was hard not to be swept up in it. Ansel kept forgetting what Brock had taught him, and started to share in the gusty excitement that was filling the hut. But when he looked at Brock he remembered. No such thing as dragons.

The press of bodies pushed him sideways, cramming him up against two girls. One was pretty, the other plain. They snatched at Ansel, eager for anything belonging to the dragon hunter. "Have you *seen* him fight dragons?" asked the pretty one, gold-haired, dimply. She had wrapped herself up in embroidery and lace and ribbons like a gift for Brock. "Were you *there*?"

"He can't answer you," said her friend, sharp-nosed and sallow. "Haven't you heard? The boy can't talk. The last dragon his master fought was so terrible that just the sight of it was enough to rob him of the power of speech."

"Poor child!" said the first, pushing Ansel's hair from his face, kneading his cheeks like dough. "Is it true?"

Ansel stared up at her, then nodded. He didn't dare deny it. He didn't know if the sharp-nosed girl had made up that detail herself or if it was something that Brock had told her. He felt as if he were drowning in lies. He pulled away from the horrible kindness of the girls and groped his way through the fog of peat smoke and the reek of bodies to the doorway.

Out he went into the night. The clouds had cleared. A hard, curved fang of moon dangled above the shoulder of the mountain. It spilled its white light down the snowfields. It glittered on the frosty ground between the huts.

Ansel let out a long breath like a plume of smoke into the chilled air and started to walk uphill towards the byre at the top of the village where Brezel and Snow were stabled beside Flegel's old nag. The thing that one of the villagers had said about the dragon ripping off a barn roof to take a cow had made him uneasy for the horses, even though he knew it had been only a story. Other stories were still being told in the hut; he could hear the blur of voices behind him as he walked.

Beyond them, down in the timber, wolves were crying, faint and far off.

He was nearing the byre when he heard another sort of cry. It was the same long, terrible sound that he had heard the night before, but it was closer now. The wolves heard it too; their howls stopped suddenly, the way birds fall silent in a wood when they hear something that frightens them. *But what would frighten a wolf?* Ansel lifted his eyes up to the hard crown of the mountain, searching among those moonwashed peaks for – what? Black wings? A belch of fiery breath? How could the dragon cry, if it was only a story?

For a moment he felt the liquid fear of yesterday gathering, rising up, ready to wash through him again. He calmed himself. *No such thing as dragons.* That's what Brock said, and who was he to doubt Johannes Brock? That yowling had just been a night bird, a wildcat, a gale of wind blustering through some hole in the rocks up there. . .

He listened, waiting for the noise to come again. It didn't. Instead he heard, from somewhere close at hand, another sound. Soft sobs and snuffles. Someone crying.

He went towards a low, half derelict hut. He'd passed it in daylight when he led the horses up, but thought it abandoned and deserted. Now, in the blue dark, he could see fire-glow lapping through chinks in its log walls. The crying came from inside, helpless, heartbroken.

Ansel lifted the flap of goatskin that covered the doorway. Smoke stung his eyes, smearing his view of the hut's interior. When he blinked the tears away he could see a woman sitting by the hearth, looking up at him in surprise through tears of her own. He couldn't tell how old she was. Not old, he thought, but her long, loose hair was greying and the winds of the mountain had tanned and lined her face. Her eyes were red-rimmed, and her nose was red too. She tried to stop her sobs when she saw him, but they kept heaving out of her, jolting her whole body.

Ansel couldn't turn away. It was as if she'd hooked him with those wet black eyes of hers.

"You came too late, you and that dragon hunter," she said. "My child's gone."

Ansel watched her mouth move, and wondered what she meant. Had the dragon taken her child? *But there's no such beast!* Was she the mother of the dead shepherd, the one Brock reckoned bandits had killed? He shook his head. *I don't understand. I can't help you.*

"They gave her to the dragon," said the woman – or rather keened it, like the starting of a song, each word one note higher than the one before it, rising to another choking sob. "I gave gold to the friar to pray for us, but they said God has deserted us, and they took her up the mountain and left her for the dragon. My baby, my child. . ."

Ansel shook his head again. He thought of the princess in that painting of St George, and tried to imagine those friendly villagers chaining a child up like that, dragging her up among the crags and leaving her there, an offering to the beast. They'd not do such things, would they? Not that kind old head man? Not those gnarled farmers and their rosy wives? But then he thought of the sly, secret looks he'd seen them give each other, and the sense he'd felt that they were hiding something. He remembered what the landgrave had said. There had been a time when Knochen village had sacrificed a girl each year to keep the dragon on the mountain quiet. If they were scared enough – and they *were* scared enough – perhaps there was *nothing* they'd not do.

So they lied too, he thought. *They didn't say a word of what they'd done. They're liars just like Brock and me.*

He wanted to comfort the woman, but he wasn't sure how. If he'd had the words he would have told her that there was no dragon, so her child was safe. But of course that wouldn't have been true. He could feel the vast cold bulk of the mountain out there in the night behind him. It was brewing up blizzards. It was dreaming of storms. He could hear the wolves again, throwing their cold voices at the moon. A child left up there might be safe from dragons, but she'd not be *safe*.

The woman started to cry again, elbows on her knees, head in her hands. Ansel backed away from her, feeling helpless in the face of her huge grief. He let the hide curtain fall and ran to the byre, burrowing into the safe, comforting warmth between the horses.

8

Before dawn he filled their saddlebags with hard black bread and dipped the water skins in the villagers' spring. At the villagers' urging Brock was taking tall ash staffs and a long, strong coil of hempen rope, and those too had to be lashed to Brezel's load. In the underwater glow of first light Ansel tightened girths and lengthened stirrups and double-knotted the bag ties. Then he went back to the head man's hut and helped the dragon slayer into his marvellous metal skin.

It didn't matter that the armour always had a scurf of rust on it, no matter how often and how carefully Ansel scrubbed and polished it. It shone in the blue dimness of the hut like a garment of light. Ansel forgave it its awkward weight and forgot the times he'd cursed it on the road, where it had been just clumsy, cumbersome baggage. He watched Brock pull on his leather cap, and then his loose coif of shining mail. He helped him into heavy, slinking sleeves, and buckled their straps across his tunic, and closed the breastplate over them. Tassets attached to the waist-flange locked in place with a sneck-hook right and left. Pauldrons fitted over Brock's shoulders, a vambrace cinched around each forearm. On his legs, for ease of movement, he wore just thick, studded breeches and his tall boots. On his head, over the fish-scale hood, went his helmet. It flashed like a halo as he stepped out on to the tramped earth in front of the hut, drawing a soft "Oh!" from the audience which had gathered there.

The villagers had dressed up too, to see the hunters on their way. They wore their festival clothes; bright tunics and bodices whose hopeful colours the half-light could not quite dim. Sunday bonnets perched like butterflies on the heads of the women and girls. As Ansel pushed past them to where he'd left the horses, they mumbled blessings at him and wished him luck. Their hands patted kindly at his shoulders and his head, but their eyes slid away when they met his. He didn't feel sorry for them any more. He wondered which of them had taken that woman's child from her and left her on the mountain.

He held the horses while Flegel flicked holy water in Brock's face and grumbled some Latin words. Then they all three mounted and rode uphill with the villagers shuffling aside to let them pass.

The bereaved woman was watching from outside her shabby hut as the hunters passed. She ran forward and reached up. "Take me with you, sirs!" Ansel heard her say, as she clutched at Brock's stirrup. "My daughter's gone to the dragon. I must find her bones and give her Christian burial."

"Pay her no mind, Brock," called Flegel. "She's mad."

Brock glanced at the woman without much interest. He jerked his foot to shake her away, and banged his heels against Snow's side, urging the mare to a brisk trot. Ansel followed, keeping his head down, ashamed to meet the woman's gaze. He noticed that Flegel did the same. Did the friar know what the villagers had done? Or was it just fear of the mountain that made him cringe like that? When he looked back, the other villagers had clustered around the widow and were guiding or forcing her back towards her hut.

When they had passed through the gate in the wall at the upper end of the village and were riding up the steep track that led between the crags above the tarn, Flegel said pettishly, "I still don't know why you had to drag me along with you."

"Because I don't trust you enough to leave you behind," said Brock. The words clanged off the flat walls of rock which rose on each side of the track, and scared up jackdaws from the overhanging bushes. "What if you blurt out my business while you're drunk on that vile beer of theirs? This way's better. And you can sing my praises to the villagers when we come down. That's the one trouble with a speechless servant like young Ansel here; he can't back up my story. But a holy friar – what better witness could I ask?"

"You are a proud and vainglorious man, Johannes Brock!" shouted Flegel. "And pride goeth before a fall! I will not follow you any higher up this accursed hill. I'm staying here!"

But Ansel knew he wouldn't. That was too desolate a place for anyone to stay alone, unless he was someone like Brock who did not fear wolves, or brigands, or the dark. He urged Brezel on uphill after his master, and when he looked back he saw that the friar was still following. The village was already far below. The gravel shallows at the edges of its tarn showed palely through the slate-coloured water. Then the track humped over a shoulder of the land and it was all hidden from view. Brock pulled off his helmet and his mail coif and slung them to Ansel to stow somehow among the rest of Brezel's cargo.

They rode on into a blustering wind, through quick falls of rain and sudden splashes of sunlight. Above them the mountain came and went, banners of cloud billowing round its summits. A stream ran down the middle of the track. Now and then there was a cross or a cairn at a bend in the way, but otherwise that country was as wild and untenanted as if no one had been there since the Creation. The hooves of the horses slithered on broad pavements of blue-grey rock that stretched across the path.

"In the beginning, the world was quite smooth,"

Flegel told them helpfully. He still kept a few scraps of knowledge from his monkish past, and he liked to share them. "A perfect sphere. It must have been, for it was the work of God, and how could a perfect God make something that was not perfect itself? But when the Devil was hurled out of Heaven he hit the earth with such a violent blow, and clawed so fiercely at it in his anguish and his rage, that it was marred and scarred. Rucked up like a rug into the horrible peaks and awful chasms we see about us. No wonder dragons and evil spirits are thought to haunt places like this. All mountains are the Devil's work."

"I like mountains," said Brock, unimpressed. "I like the silence of them. So stop your chatter, and save your breath."

They reached a place where the track narrowed to a stony shelf. On their right side, like a wall, a cliff went up into mist. On their left, a precipice dropped away sheer into a chasm filled with tumbled shards of rock the size of castle towers. A white river thundered down in the bottom of that gorge, filling the air with fine spray and a steady, ominous roaring. They dismounted and led the horses along the path, still climbing steadily, Brock at the front, Flegel in the middle, Ansel coaxing the nervy Brezel along behind. The friar grumbled ceaselessly. "This is as bad as fighting dragons! We'll break our necks! The horses will bolt and drag us to our doom! This isn't fair, Brock! This is madness! Mountains weren't made to be climbed, and men weren't made to climb them."

"Petrarch climbed Mount Ventoux, I've heard," said Brock. "Moses climbed Sinai. Didn't Christ himself go up a mountain?"

"Yes, and the Devil sat on the top and showed him all the kingdoms of the earth. I don't want to meet the Devil. We've gone far enough, Brock, haven't we? Can't we stop now?"

A curl of black cloud came over the mountain high above them, and the wind howled. Hail came down at them like slingshots, and there was nowhere to shelter. The horses skittered, shoes sparking on the rock at the brim of that appalling drop. Over the crackle of the hail Brock shouted, "The villagers told me of a high pasture, with a shepherd's shelter built beneath an overhang of rock. That'll serve as our lodgings. It can't be far now. . ."

The hail passed. The sun came out and drew the shadows of men and boy and horses on the rocks. They crept on, up and up, past a black and shattered-looking crag from which great stones had fallen in the past and now lay scattered down a steep slope of scree that looked ready to slide down and sweep the travellers off the path. But once they were past it the path widened, and led them away from the cliff's edge at last and up on to a ridge where whitish grass hissed in the wind. Beyond the ridge lay a bowl of high grassland, patched with the shadows of clouds. Around its edges there were bogs, and pools of water shone out here and there amid the grass like little slices cut from the sky and dropped upon the mountain. A stunted tree grew by the track where it curved down into the valley, and there were ropes tied round some of the lower branches, a few frayed ends flapping in the wind.

Ansel thought at once of the girl they'd brought up here to give to the dragon. Was that where they'd left her? Tied to that tree? But where had she gone? What could have cut through those thick ropes and taken her?

For a moment the dragon fear lurched up in him again, and he wanted to get Brock's attention and show him those ropes. But Brock and the friar were already moving on, down the grassy slope into the meadow. Brock was pointing ahead, towards the wall of rock which barred the head of the valley. At its foot, among the mounds of boulders piled there by nature, a few courses of laid stones showed. A haze of smoke hung there.

"That's the shepherd's shelter," said Brock.

"There's a fire!" said Flegel nervously. "Someone's here before us!"

Brock laughed. "Or perhaps it's dragon's smoke. . ."

They climbed on to the horses again. There was a slough in the bottom of the valley where the mud came up to Brezel's knees, but apart from that the going was easy. Bones lay in the dry beige grass; the long, knobbled spine of a sheep with its splayed-out ribs like the tines of a white rake.

"Not your handiwork, I suppose?" said Brock.

"Of course not!" replied Flegel. "Do you think I'd climb all the way up here to murder sheep? I told you I killed only two, and they were down by the village. A wolf took this one."

The shepherd's shelter was a natural cave, across the mouth of which a loose wall of dry stones had been piled up. An old wooden beam dragged up from the village made a lintel above the doorway, and a hide hung from it to keep out the cold.

Someone had wedged two more old timbers across the doorway in an X shape, like a barricade.

The riders reined in outside. Something moved behind the hide curtain. A scuffling sound. A cloud hid the sun, sudden as a door shutting, and a cold wind touched the back of Ansel's neck.

Brock swung himself down out of Snow's saddle and went to the doorway. He kicked away the barriers, pulled open the curtain, and jumped back with a grunt of surprise.

In the low doorway a girl crouched, watching him. Her eyes were wide and mad and she bared her small yellow teeth at Brock like a cornered dog. In her hand there was a knife.

9

"Christ's bones!" said Brock. "Who's this?"

No one answered him, so he snatched the knife out of the girl's hand and dragged her aside and flung her on the grass while he went inside the shelter. A girl of twelve or thirteen summers, dressed in the remnants of the same bright Sunday garments the girls in the village had worn. A broken-winged butterfly bonnet came loose from her hair as she fell on the ground and the wind took it up, up, up over the crags and away.

Brock came out of the hut with the girl's small knife still in his hand. "Those fools!" he said. "They left her here. Like a gift for the worm. Sweet Christ! The landgrave spoke to me of this. Of how in pagan times they'd leave a maiden on the mountain as a sacrifice. But I didn't believe they'd really do it!"

"I *knew* they were keeping secrets from me," said Flegel, trying to sound as if the truth was just dawning on him. The girl had sat up, staring at the dragon hunters. Flegel flinched when he met her eye, as if her look burned.

Brock lifted the girl's arms and looked at the rope bites on her thin wrists. "They tethered her to the tree over there," he said. "They didn't wait to see if the worm came for her, just ran back to Knochen. Lucky for her she had that knife about her. She must have managed to cut the ropes through, and came and hid in here."

"Can't she talk for herself then?" asked Flegel. "Is she another dumb one, like your boy here?"

"She's scared," said Brock. There was a stillness about him, as he looked down at the girl, that Ansel hadn't seen before. All those years of make-believe dragon hunts, the easy routine of it, and now, here, he had found something different at last. He was probably wondering how he would fit the girl into his plans.

"You'll die," said the girl suddenly, surprising them all. The wind gusted, smelling of rain, lifting the corners of her soot-black hair. She said, "If you stay here, you'll die. The dragon will come."

"There is nothing to fear," said Brock.

"Brock's a mighty dragon slayer," said Flegel. "Look at his armour, and that sword he wears. He's God's soldier, appointed to rid this mountain of its monster."

The girl looked sceptically at the armour and the sword. "Those won't do any good," she said. "It's too big. It come last night. In the twilight. I heard it growling and rubbing its sides against the wall."

"A wolf, I dare say," said Brock. "She heard a wolf, and thought it was the worm."

"I've seen wolves before," the girl said doggedly. "I know wolves, and this weren't no wolf. I saw its eye peer in at me between the stones. I smelled its breath."

"It can't have stunk any worse than she does," said Flegel uncharitably. But it was true, the reek of stale fear came off the girl; sweat and urine had soaked into her tattered finery and mingled with the smell of the uncured sheepskins she'd wrapped herself in against the cold.

Flegel turned to Brock and Ansel. "She's mad. Yes, I recall her now. They pointed her out to me in the village the day I arrived. She's the brat of that shepherd who vanished on the mountain. Her mother's crazy, and she's worse. You can't believe anything she tells you. Do you think they would have left her up here if she were whole and sound? She's mad, and that's why they chose her for their sacrifice."

"You didn't try to stop them, then?"

"I didn't know!" the friar said squeakily. "She was there when I came, and then she was gone. I knew they were agitated about something; I knew they were keeping secrets, but I had no notion of what wickedness they had worked!"

He *had* known, though. He'd known all along. You could hear the guilt in his voice and see it peeking out from inside his hurt, angry eyes.

"What are we going to do with her, Brock?" he asked.

Brock looked at him. His nostrils flared. Up above the mountain, thunder shuddered and rain came spattering down. "We'd best get us inside," he said. "Bring the horses too. It won't do to leave them out here if there are wolves about."

Ansel coaxed the horses in through the door in the wall. The front part of the cave was broad and high-roofed. A kind of pound had been made there for animals, separated off by a lower wall from the shepherd's quarters at the back, where the cave roof sloped down to meet the floor, black with the smoke and soot of many fires. Ansel tethered the horses and went back outside to fetch water for them in a leathern bucket while Brock made Flegel and the girl help him carry the baggage deeper in.

By the time Ansel hurried back from the stream the rain was coming on, veils of it swaying over the valley and falling on the grass with a hard hiss. The thunder banged like slammed doors, echoing about between the crags. The rain turned to hail again and they crammed together into the back of the cave, coughing on the smoke from the heather-root fire which was burning in the stone hearth. A stack of uncured sheepskins lay piled in a corner.

"I don't like this," Flegel grumbled. "I don't like it at all. There was no need to come so high, Brock. What if a tempest of snow comes down and traps us here? We have only food for two days. What will we eat? And what about the girl? She'll spoil your plan, won't she? What will we *do* with her?"

Brock watched the girl. The fire gleamed in his armour and on his silvery-smooth scar and in his dark, secretive eyes. He was remembering all the tales of chivalry he'd heard when he was a boy. How he'd dreamed of one day being one of those shining knights who won battles and rescued maidens from giants and monsters. Those dreams hadn't stayed long, of course. One glimpse of a real battle had knocked them straight out of his head. But now, finding himself suddenly the protector of this snivelling, shivering girl, they came sneaking back. Slaying imaginary worms and tricking mountain villagers out of their small savings wasn't the sort of job that made a man proud of himself. But if he could save this child from the mountain and her credulous neighbours, that would be a sort of chivalry, wouldn't it?

"Why did they bring you up here?" he asked the girl. "Why you, out of all the village girls?"

The girl gave an unhappy shrug. She kept her eyes on the earth floor while she answered. "They said my father woke the dragon, or angered it, or something. He said there weren't no such thing as dragons. He said it must be some great bird or something that laired up here, and gave rise to so many tales. He went climbing all over the mountain, looking for its nest. And one time he went up and never came down again. And soon after that the sheep started being killed, and people heard the dragon howling, and everyone said it was Father's fault. Said he'd gone into its lair and woken it and now it wouldn't sleep till it had eaten of the flesh of his flesh. That's me, see. Mother tried to stop them taking me. She prayed that Friar would stop them. She thought they'd listen to him. She *paid* him to stop them. But he didn't."

"It's lies!" squeaked Flegel. "Don't you see? She's stark mad, and now she's twisting me into her stories!"

The girl shrugged. "He couldn't have stopped them anyway," she said. "They fear the dragon more than God now. They're wild with the fear of it."

"There are no such things as dragons," said Brock gently.

"Oh, there is, sir," said the girl. (And if Ansel hadn't known better he'd have believed her, the sure way she said it. He had to remind himself that Brock knew better than a mad mountain-peasant girl.) "I *saw* it," she said. "I saw its cold old eye look in at me through that chink in the wall. Yellow it was. Like a cold flame."

Suddenly, from outside the cave, there came a terrible roar, deeper and longer-lasting than the thunder. It made the cave floor tremble. It shook small pebbles down from the roof. Everyone started up, confused by the sound and by the frightened stamping and snorting of the horses. Brock grabbed his sword. Flegel crossed himself, mumbling prayers. Ansel imagined great scaled feet pulling the stones of the crags asunder; a dreadful head nosing towards the smell of people and horses. In the front part of the cave the horses whickered, barging against each other in their fear, knocking a stone from the low wall which separated their lodgings from the humans' quarters.

Outside, for an appallingly long time, the roaring and tumbling and rattling rolled on and on, fading slowly to a last bounding clatter, a final crunch.

"Landslide, over among the crags somewhere," said Brock, relaxing. He grinned at the girl. "This is a hard old mountain, but there's no worm on it. It was a wolf that peeked in at you, my dear. So we'd best prop those baulks of timber across the door again, and keep that fire alight."

10

Her name was Else, and it had come as no real
surprise to her when she found herself being
marched up the mountain by her neighbours
and tethered to a tree as dragon food. Her luck
had turned bad before she was even born, and
it showed no sign yet of ever coming good
again.

First there was her mother: not a village woman
but a travelling tinker from over the mountain

somewhere, dark as a Turk. From her, Else got her black, unruly hair and those thick black eyebrows that met across the top of her nose.

Then there was her father. A kind enough man, and he knew the mountains better than anyone, but too thoughtful; ideas sprouted in his head like weeds and left no room in there for common sense. Everyone knew they were a bad-luck family, and when he vanished on the mountain that just confirmed it. They started to keep clear of Else and her mother, just in case the bad luck rubbed off on them. The blue-eyed woodcutter's boy from the village down the valley, who used to pay so much attention to her when she went down with her mother to church, wouldn't even look at her after that. She heard the other girls talking about her. They were remembering how strange she was, how she fell into daydreams and fancies. How, when she was smaller, she'd come down delighted from watching the sheep on the mountain and said she'd seen angels blowing past in the sunlight, high over the crags.

After her father died, there was no one to help when the winds of January tore off half the roof. Out in the cold on a ladder, making repairs as best she could with her numb, blue fingers, Else could feel her neighbours' eyes on her. She could feel their thoughts worming towards her at night, when the dragon's cries rebounded off the crags and men lay awake wondering whose sheep, whose cattle would be found ripped and gutted in the morning.

She knew why they looked at her. She knew what they were thinking. If blood had to be spilled again to quieten the dragon, like it used to be in the olden days, if someone had to be offered up to the restless and hungry spirit of the mountain, then who better than the daughter of the man who'd woken it? Flesh of his flesh, blood of his blood. Who else but Else?

When the friar arrived she'd thought at first it might be all right. Her mother had given him gold to make him stay in the village, the same fat gold coins she'd once brought to Else's father as a dowry. She'd told her neighbours, too loudly and too confidently, that the holy man's prayers would drive the dragon back into its hole. And they'd welcomed him, of course. They were glad of help from any quarter, any god, by then. But it hadn't stopped them glancing sideways at Else, or holding those quick, muttered conclaves that went quiet when she walked by. It hadn't stopped them barging in through the door curtain one morning while Brother Flegel was sleeping off the feast they'd fed him, and dragging Else away. The women trussed her in her Sunday clothes, and the men carried her like a parcel away up the mountain, as high as they dared. There, on the high pasture, they'd roped her to that tree and left her.

And right till that moment, when they tugged the knots tight and scurried away, too ashamed of themselves to say anything or even meet her eye, right until then Else had half thought that it really *was* her fault. She wasn't clever. She lived in the village like a fish lives in water, knowing nothing else. If all her neighbours blamed the dragon on her father and said her death would be the thing to quiet it, well, they must be right, mustn't they? That was why she hadn't screamed or bitten or struggled when they came for her, and why she'd felt so oddly ashamed at her mother's struggling, her mother's screams.

But up there on the mountain, with the hard bones of the tree digging into her back and the ropes gnawing her wrists and the wind booming past her, she'd started to wonder. She couldn't have deserved *this*, could she? She squinted into the sun as it rose over the crags and watched the sky for dragon wings. A queasy question started nagging at her. What would it *feel* like, to be eaten?

Moments like that, in stories, were when the handsome prince came riding up to slay the beast, save the maiden and carry her home to his castle. But there was a shortage of handsome princes up that mountain. And if one had happened by, his white charger would have snapped its dainty ankles on the screes, and he would hardly have bothered unsheathing his shining sword to save an unbeautiful farm girl like Else. If she was to be rescued, she reckoned she would have to rescue herself.

So she wriggled and writhed till one hand came free of the rope. She fumbled her little short knife out of the pocket of her shirt. She used it for cutting switches when she was minding the sheep, but it worked on ropes as well, eventually, though it took such a time for the blade to gnaw through the damp hemp that she was sure the dragon would be upon her before she was finished. Sawing at the rope round her ankles, she kept expecting to look up and find it watching her, patient, claws crossed, stifling a yawn.

But it wasn't.

Pounding across the squelchy pastures to the shepherd's shelter, stumbling over the bones of butchered sheep, she expected wingbeats, a sun-blotting shadow, and then the claws like meat hooks driven through her, yanking her into the sky.

But they never came.

She reached the shelter, ran inside, and crouched there in the shadows, shivering. She had been there ever since. She had made a fire from the heap of heather roots which was piled up in a corner, and eaten the sour brown apples which some herdsman had stored there in the autumn and forgotten to take down with him when winter closed the high pastures. She listened to the wind and the sounds of the mountain. She listened to the dragon slithering about outside, waiting for her to come out.

Was it real, or was it something not-quite-real? Not *really* real, like those gorgeous, golden angels she'd seen when she was a little girl, dancing on the wind above the mountain? She couldn't be certain, so she decided it would be safest never to leave the cave again.

Now she kept to her corner, watching Johannes Brock and his wordless boy build the fire up, watching the pitiful Father Flegel try not to meet her eyes. She had wondered at first if Brock might count as one of those handsome princes. But he wasn't that handsome and he wasn't a prince and although that sword of his looked fine and shiny, she didn't think it would make a dent in anything as big as the beast she'd heard in the night, rubbing its armoured flanks against the outsides of the shelter.

But she was glad he was there all the same, him and his ragtag group of followers.

Because maybe when it came back the beast would eat one of *them*, instead of her.

She slept, and Brock watched her. He was wondering what he should do with her. If he took her back with him to Knochen, she'd give the game away for sure, and tell the villagers he'd killed no worm upon their high pastures.

If he had been another sort of man he would have made sure she never left the mountain. It would be easy enough to cut her throat and bury her deep under scree stones, where no one would find her bones. To say, if anybody ever asked, that the dragon must have eaten her. But Johannes Brock had never done violence to anyone. As a young man, riding to his first war, he had dreamed of striking down God's enemies left and right, but when he actually found himself in the middle of that battle, smelling the blood and hearing the cries of the hurt and dying all around him, something changed in him. He couldn't use his sword, not even to defend himself. He only survived that fight because no blade or arrow tip pierced his armour.

Afterwards he rode away alone, too shaken to face his comrades or ever to return to his own lands and explain his cowardice to his family. He'd become a wanderer instead, and turned at last to dragon hunting, fighting enemies who never bled or cried for mercy, mainly because they didn't exist. So he did not even think of silencing Else with his knife.

Anyway, he decided, it would be impressive, wouldn't it, to bring her back down to Knochen? Maybe she would go along with his story. She had no reason to love her neighbours, after what they'd done. Perhaps she'd be glad to help him deceive them.

The girl was sleeping now. Ansel too, and Flegel of course, snoring like a wood saw. The horses slept standing, heads hanging down. Brock wrapped his travelling cloak a little tighter round him and pillowed his head on the saddlebag with its swaddled skull and soon he was sleeping too.

If anything bellowed that night, prowling outside upon the mountain, it went unheard amid the louder bellowing of the storm.

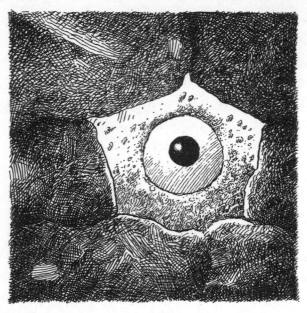

11

Ansel awoke to the restless snorting and whinnying of the horses. No sound of wind. Grey morning light seeped through the chinks in the wall at the cave mouth. The tempest had blown itself out in the night.

He sat up. The others sprawled about the hearth where they had fallen asleep. Flegel was still snoring wetly, bundled so deep in skins and blankets that only his red boots showed. The girl called Else had squirmed herself into an alcove in the cave wall and tugged a fleece across it, to keep the cold out or hide herself from dragons' eyes, or Brock's and Flegel's, or all three.

Ansel got up and stretched. He mumbled his morning prayer. The stones he had slept upon had filled his body with nagging aches. He needed to piss, but Else being there made him shy, even though she was asleep. What if she woke?

At the front of the cave the horses stamped and snorted fretfully, tugging at their tethers. Ansel supposed that a cave was not a natural place for them. He went to calm them, slapping their necks, smoothing his hand down their long velvet noses. They nudged and nuzzled him, and ate up the bunches of dry grass he held out for them, but they stayed nervous. He went past them, pulled the door curtain aside, nervously checked the world outside for waiting wolves, and went out.

Sunlight lay on the meadow and on all the crags that watched over it. At some point in the night the rain had turned to snow. Swags and slashes of it lay about on the brown grass, almost too bright to look at. Higher up, on the crags and on the ridges above them, everything was dazzling white. The world felt fresh-made.

Ansel walked in among a tumble of large boulders which lay a short way off. Ravens rose from a sheep carcass and circled, cawing. Their shadows went flicking over the stones while Ansel opened his breeches and watched the steamy yellow stream go winding downhill between his boots. He was just lacing himself up again when a stone fell somewhere behind him, racketing down from rock to rock across the face of one of the crags which ringed the valley. It was followed by a spattering rush of dislodged snow. Ansel looked round without thinking. His eyes went up and up a mossy cliff, up to the sharp summit where the stone had come from.

An animal was perched there, watching him.

Ansel stared at the creature and tried to find a word for it. He tried to make its shape fit the shapes of creatures he had seen before. *Lizard? Bird? Maybe it's a corkindrille? Maybe it's nothing but a trick my eyes are playing?*

(*It's a dragon*, said his heart, stilled to a whisper inside him. But there were no such things as dragons.)

It didn't look a bit like the skull in Brock's bag. Its head was a short, brutal blade, freckled with hard black scales, the spiny ridges over its eyes as rough as pine cones. A pulse throbbed in the soft leather folds of its snaky throat. Its body was as big as the body of a small horse, and armoured all over in scales. The scales were longer on its shoulders and flanks and wings. They were so long that they weren't really scales at all, but feathers, ruffling silently in the wind. The wings were folded up close under its chest, and at the end of each wing three blue-black talons glittered like dark glass. The larger talons of its feet clutched the rock's edge.

"*It's a dragon*," Ansel's body told him. "*It's a dragon*," said each hair on the nape of his neck, bristling.

A growl bubbled softly, deep in the soundbox of the creature's chest. The eye it aimed at him was sulphur yellow. It opened its mouth, and its teeth were icicle white and sharp as nails and its tongue was a pink spike. As it launched itself off the crag towards him, Ansel saw the long tail lash out behind it, striped like a serpent and frilled with feathers.

He ran backwards through the rocks, stumbling, scattering sheep bones, bleached ribs crunching under his boots. He turned and fled uphill towards the shelter. He could hear the thing coming after him. The wind whirred in those weird feathers. A mad shadow swept over him and spread black wings across the shelter wall as he threw himself through the low door, letting the curtain of hide flump shut behind him. He fell forward into a confusion of rearing, neighing horses, maddened by the fierce scent that Ansel had brought in with him.

"Ansel?" said Brock, awake, heaving himself upright, rubbing at the bruises of the night.

Something hit the front of the shelter like a storm of wind; scrabbling claws and a rasp of scales on stone and a long, bitter screech of animal frustration.

"Christ!" Brock shouted. He reached down for his sword and started tugging it out of its scabbard. Flegel came awake too, demanding to know what was happening. Else's eyes peeked out from the shadows of her hiding hole. The horses screamed, and something else screamed too, a hard, jagged scream, like some huge and evil bird.

"What in Christ's name was that?" asked Brock stupidly, sword out, back against the wall.

"A wolf?" asked Flegel, almost hopeful.

"*Dragon!*" mouthed Ansel, scrambling up amid the stamping hooves, the spattering dung. He flapped his arms like wings in a frantic mime. He tried to show them its huge jaws, and its claws, and its feathered tail. "*DRAGON!*" But Brock and Flegel didn't understand him. Only the horses knew, barging and jostling him as they turned this way and that, desperate to escape the cave as it filled with dragon-scent. Brezel pulled free of his tether and pushed deeper inside, knocking Ansel down again.

Something hard was grating along the outside of the shelter wall. The bars of daylight that raked in through the chinks between the stones were put out one by one. Between the shrieks of the horses, Brock's steady cursing and the querulous demands from Flegel, Ansel thought he heard loud, snorting breaths. He crouched in the hoof-trodden mud and dung behind the wall, and saw that sulphur-yellow eye stare in at him through a gap between two stones. The black pupil widened as the creature looked into the shadows of the cave. Ansel, nailed by a beam of sunlight slanting through a higher opening, saw his own face mirrored in it, and the answering blackness of his wide and wordless mouth.

Like a mailed fist banging on a door, the hungry creature slammed itself against the wall of stones. The stones shifted, grating against each other. Scraps of dried moss, stuffed into crannies long ago to keep the weather out, came feathering down around Ansel where he crouched. He couldn't move. He felt as if he had grown roots. He could only wait there, watching, while the creature drew itself back and struck again. Harder this time. The whole wall wobbled. A largish stone, sprung from near the top, thudded into the mud not far from Ansel. Sunlight dazzled through the gap it left. The next blow dislodged a little avalanche of stones which rattled down the outside of the wall, and the beast outside jumped back, snarling.

A strong hand held Ansel's arm and hauled him bodily backwards. He looked up. Brock.

"What's out there, Ansel? What is it really?"

"*Dragon!*"

Brock understood him that time. Maybe he'd already guessed, so it was easier for him to read the word in the shape Ansel's mouth made. He looked towards the cave-mouth, brighter now with those stones gone from the wall's top. "It can't be," he said. "It can't be! There is no such beast. . ."

The dragon seemed to want to prove him wrong, for it chose that moment to thrust its head in through the curtained entrance. Its eyes were as big as eggs, as yellow as yolks. Its mouth opened unbelievably wide, and its voice filled the cave.

Ansel crammed his hands over his ears. He saw Flegel do the same. At the back of the cave, the girl Else was a shuddering huddle under her sheepskin. When the roaring stopped Ansel could hear her screaming, a thinner, higher sound than the sound of the horses. Flegel's gelding had snapped its tether now, and he and Brezel were pushing as deep into the cave as they could, heads up and ears back and eyes wide and white.

Brock's mare Snow turned circles on her halter, kicking out at the dragon with her hooves. She caught it a blow on its scaly nose that jolted its head sideways. It hissed in pain and snapped at her, but couldn't reach; its body was too big to fit through the entrance. It pulled back, and the hide curtain flopped down into place again.

For a moment all was quiet, or at least quieter. Snow snorted and stamped. Flegel whimpered. Else stopped screaming and peeked her eyes over the edge of the fleece that hid her with a look in them that said, *I told you so.* Brock looked at his sword, as if he were measuring it against the dragon's armoury of hooked teeth.

"You told me there were no such things as dragons, Brock," Flegel was saying sullenly. "You said there were no such things. . ."

Brock shook himself. He was very white, and the sword he was holding shook steadily in time to the shaking of his hands. In a quiet, wondering way he said, "They were telling the truth. Those villagers. They weren't the fools we thought."

"But you said—"

The dragon drove itself against the wall like a battering ram. Sunlight splashed in as the big stones fell. One hit Snow just above the root of her tail and she collapsed, whinnying shrilly, struggling to rise on legs that would not work. The dragon thrust its head and forequarters in through the gap it had made. Brock ran at it, cursing, brandishing his sword, but Flegel's horse, rearing up in terror, knocked him sideways with its flailing hooves. The dragon's jaws scissored shut on Snow's neck. Her head plunged, wild-eyed, snorting out bloody foam. The dragon snapped her spine with a quick, irritable twitch of its head. She shuddered, and grew suddenly heavy and slack, head lolling and legs tangling as the beast wrestled her back through the wreck of the wall.

Brock scrambled up and shouted something. He waved his sword.

Flegel was on his feet too, maybe reasoning that he was safe till the beast finished devouring Brock's mare. He raised his hand, two fingers crooked, two raised in blessing, calling on God and His Saints to smite the evil one.

The dragon took no notice of either of them. It dragged the dead mare a little way downhill and perched prissily over her, holding its long tail out stiffly behind it for balance as it started to eat. It tore the carcass open with its claws and jaws and stuffed its greedy head inside. Snow's innards steamed in the sunlight.

Brock scrambled over the tumble of stones which had been the wall. Ansel ran to the saddlebags and fetched his coif and helmet, then went after him, very scared, but wanting to see what would happen. He pushed the mail and helmet at his master, and Brock grunted and took them and crammed them on his head without ever taking his eyes from the dragon. He walked forward, and Ansel watched. The dragon stopped eating for a moment and looked up at them. Its face was a red knife. Brock and Ansel didn't seem to interest it. It went back to its meal, and its crunchings and slurpings echoed off the cliffs above the cave.

"That's my horse!" shouted Brock. "That's my horse, you worm!"

He ran downhill, his armour a mirror, all sunshine and blood. The sword swung up to strike. The dragon, with an exasperating, lazy grace, hopped away. One flap of those unlikely feathered wings carried it twenty feet. It crouched on a rock, head low, tail out like a battle lance, big armoured feet set wide apart. It roared, and its bellow slammed off the cliffs and raised crows from the crags a mile away.

Brock ran at it again. This time it flapped towards him. The flash of the sword frightened it and it veered aside without biting him, but its tail came round hard and struck him across the shoulders, throwing him down into the grass.

"Brock!" shouted Flegel, watching from just inside the cave.

Brock rolled over in the grass. He had dropped the sword. Ansel ran to where it lay. He picked it up, surprised at its weight, and dragged it to where Brock was getting up. "Good boy," said the dragon hunter, taking it, pushing Ansel behind him. But the dragon had lost interest in them again. Long-legged, folding its wings and bringing its clawed hands up against its chest, it stalked back to its prey. Ansel and his master stood and watched as it tore at the mare's carcass, sometimes lifting its head to gulp down a morsel, sometimes watching them with those yellow eyes. Once it paused and lifted its tail and let out a loud fart. When there was nothing much left of poor Snow but bones and sinews and her hollowed hide it suddenly took flight, flapping away across the valley. It flew clumsily, like a thing not made for flying. After each beat of its wings it seemed about to fall, until another thick, effortful beat heaved it upwards again. At last it was hidden from them by the bald crags.

Ansel looked at Brock. Brock looked at Ansel. For once the dragon hunter seemed as dumb as his servant. Into their silence fell the hard voices of the ravens which were wafting down to pick at the dragon's leavings.

12

Brock shoved his sword into the ground and sat down beside it, all the straps and buckles of his armour creaking. Ansel went a little way away and was sick into the blowing grass. He was feeling dizzy and light-headed. Even walking felt strange. The valley, the mountain, all looked as it had the day before, but the world was changed. He'd never *really* believed in dragons. Even before Brock shared his secrets, when Ansel had felt so fearful of the dragons he claimed to hunt, he hadn't really *believed*. He'd imagined Brock's dragons as being the way dragons were in stories. He hadn't imagined the stink of one, the jut and ripple of all the bones and muscles working under its hide, its animal presence.

A feather blew across the ground to him. It was not a crow's. Too long, too hard, too tapering. The quill that had rooted it to the dragon's flesh was black, and hard as flint. In all his life, he'd neither heard nor dreamed of dragon feathers.

Flegel came running past him, looking up at the sky to make sure the beast was not coming back. "Brock!" he shouted. "Brock! It was *real*! You said such things were just in stories!"

Brock looked up at him. "I thought they were," he said. "I never. . ." He looked towards the crags where the worm had vanished. He was doing what Ansel had done when it first appeared, trying to force the creature in his memory into the shape of some other, more natural beast: a lizard or a huge bird. But it would not fit. Not even he, Johannes Brock, who had wandered in far-off countries and dukes' menageries and seen spotted cameleopards and armoured unicorns, had ever seen a thing like that outside a picture. He shook his head, numbly rebuilding his world around this new truth. "It was a *dragon*, Ansel! Merciful Christ, it was a *real, live worm*! It ate Snow! Poor Snow. . ."

They stood and looked wonderingly at the place where the creature had squatted; at the mare's splayed wreckage and the blood soaking into the ground.

"I wonder why it didn't breathe its fire on us?" asked Brock.

"Because I cowed it with my prayers," said Flegel. "It would have savaged you for sure, if it had not heard me calling upon Christ and the Holy Virgin."

"So it was *you* who saved *me*?" Brock glanced at him. "I wonder you didn't call upon Our Lord to strike it dead, while you were at it."

"There is only so much, Brock, only so much a sinner like me can do against the powers of the Evil One. Oh, Brock, let us go down off this mountain before it returns!"

"Go down?" Brock seemed barely to be listening. He was feeling a sort of excitement he hadn't known since he was a young man, hurrying off to the wars with his head stuffed full of stories. One by one he'd proved them to be lies. Chivalry and love and the goodness of God, none of them were more than idle tales, told by fools to keep their fears at bay. And he'd thought monsters were just stories too, until he saw his dragon. He stood and watched the crags that had hidden it and he thought, *I faced it. I am not a coward. I faced it, and if I met it again, when I was ready for it, I could kill it. I could avenge poor Snow. I could really be Brock the worm slayer at last.* And it was like a strange, sweet, half-remembered taste to think of his sword in the beast's heart. Was this God's plan for him? He looked back quickly over all the accidents and bad decisions which had led him to this moment and this particular mountain, and wondered if there had been a meaning to it after all. Johannes Brock, Christ's champion against the Powers of Evil. . .

"Brock?" said the friar.

He looked round. He said, "It caught me off guard. I shall be ready for it next time."

"Next time?" wailed Flegel, hopping from foot to foot, sweaty with fear. "Brock, we have escaped its jaws once, with the good Lord's help. It would be folly to go seeking it again! Let us go down off this accursed mountain. Find yourself a few strong men in the foothills if you want to fight the creature."

Brock considered that. "A lance would be

useful," he admitted. "Or a heavy spear, the sort you'd use for boar. Wolfhounds to track it, and men to help me skin it, or to drag the carcass down. . ."

"A most wise notion!" said Flegel, eagerly. "Come back with hunters and hounds and wagons. Bring priests. Bring the bishop. Bring an army if you must. But don't bring me! Let's go down, Brock."

But Brock just stood there, staring at the crags. "The stories were true, Flegel," he said. "They were all true. . ."

Ansel left them and walked back to the shelter, looking up frequently all the way. He would never trust the sky again. He tried not to think about Snow. He thought instead of the girl, Else, whom Brock should have believed. She had not yet emerged from the shelter. Ansel picked his way over the wrecked wall and went to the back of the cave, reaching out to pat and stroke the two shuddering horses who were hiding there, crammed as close to the rear wall as the low roof would let them. When they were calm enough to let him past he found Else looking warily at him out of her hole.

"I told you it was real," she said.

Ansel flapped his hands and pointed, trying to

show her that the dragon had gone. She knew that anyway, from the way Brock and Flegel were talking outside and no one was being eaten, but she stayed where she was. Every time she blinked she could see that angry, open mouth with its lines of teeth. The dragon had branded itself on her eyes like the sun.

After a while Flegel and Brock came back into the cave. It seemed that Flegel had won the argument. "We're going down," said Brock, and stood at the cave mouth, watching the crags, while Ansel hurried about rolling blankets and stowing bags. Saddling the horses seemed to calm them a little; they did not shy too much when he led them outside. A flake of black swooped overhead, making him cower, but it was only a crow.

With Snow gone, Brock would ride Flegel's horse, and Flegel would ride Brezel. Ansel didn't bother feeling bitter about being made to walk. He was only a servant, after all, and that was the way of things. All he cared about was getting off the mountain. He went back into the cave to let Else know that they were leaving. She watched him doubtfully while he mimed riding and drew the steep downward road in the air with his hands. At last he coaxed her out.

"Why don't you speak?" she said.

Ansel didn't have a mime for that. He shrugged, and spread his palms.

Else sneezed. Squeezing into that cranny had left her bruised and grazed. The damp felt of her ruined festival clothes seemed stiff as armour. She flinched from Ansel's touch when he reached out to help her over the stone tumble. Didn't he know she was a mountain girl who'd been clambering over clitters and screes long before he was even born? Maybe he was simple as well as silent. . .

In her irritation she almost forgot the dragon until she was over the stones and stood blinking in the sunshine. She had forgotten how wide the sky was. You couldn't watch all of it, not all the time, could you? And even if you could, there were so many crags and clouds for a dragon to hide behind. . .

She shuddered, and then, wanting Ansel to think it was just the cold, she wrapped herself in a fleece which she had brought with her from inside the cave, knotting the ends across her chest like a shawl. The wind stirred the greasy wool. She imagined the breeze carrying her scent to the nostrils of the dragon, wherever the dragon was.

It would return, she knew that. Now that it had

found food in the cave, it would be back for more. Better to go down the mountain with the hunter and his boy and the fat friar. Better to go down the mountain with their horses. The dragon would take the horses first, and then the men. There was a chance, with all of them to distract it, that she might get back to her mother's house alive.

What she would do then, where they would go, she couldn't think. There wasn't room in her head for thoughts like that, while she was on the mountain. Up here the dragon coiled heavily in her brain, and left no space to think of anything except how to escape it, and what it would be like if she didn't. How it would feel to be seized and torn into pieces, like that poor horse. . .

Brock and Flegel had not waited. They were already riding downhill. Else and Ansel hurried after them, glancing up at the crags as they went, afraid of every shadow and each odd, sunlit rock. But Ansel told himself that the dragon had fed. Now that Snow was in its belly it might sleep for hours, maybe for days. From what he'd seen of it, the beast was just a big, fierce animal. He'd looked into its eyes, and seen nothing but hunger there. It had shown no sign of wit, or power of speech. It was not some magic mountain monster. Not

Lucifer in a lizardy disguise. Just an animal, and that meant that he could guess at how it would behave. It couldn't be so very different from a dog or a cat or the old mangy dancing bear that showmen had brought to his father's tavern that time. It would sleep when it had fed.

But he could not think of a way to tell Else that without using words.

They caught up with the riders down in the valley's miry bottom, where runnels of water rilled through the bog grass. Else scrambled across the wet places from rock to rock, and Ansel followed her, while the nervous horses wallowed knee-deep, their hooves belching and sucking in the black muck. Together they went towards the ridge and the lone tree where Else's neighbours had tied her. They were so busy watching the heights above them that they didn't notice the tree was gone.

13

Ansel was the first to guess what had happened. He ran ahead of the others, up the steep bend of the sheep track to the place where the tree had stood. The tree was gone, and so was half the crag which had towered behind it. Bare wet soil and tumbled rocks were strewn all down the mountainside. Deep drifts of loose stones, including a granite boulder the size of a small ship, had buried that shelf-wide path which they had crept along the day before.

It surprised him that a mountain could alter so, and in so short a time. He'd always thought of mountains as being dependable things, hard and unchanging. But water and ice had been working at the rocks of the crag since the world was new-made, and last night's rain had finished the job. *A landslide*, thought Ansel, recalling all the crashing and clattering they had heard in the night.

"I don't think God wants us to leave this mountain," said Brock, reining in Flegel's horse and studying the stones which barred their way. He didn't sound alarmed, simply intrigued.

"It's not God's mountain!" Flegel said. "This is Satan's work! He wants to feed us to his serpent!"

Ansel looked at the huge rock barring their path. Flegel said, "We'll never get the horses over that."

"We'll lead them round it, then," said Brock.

Above the big rock, tumbled stones and smaller boulders and masses of loose, wet earth stretched steeply upwards. Roots stuck out of the ground, and little streams were starting to find their way down, cutting gulleys for themselves through the spoil. Ansel imagined leading Brezel and the other horse up that slithery slope, and down again on the far side. Once they were past the rock they would be on the path again. But could it be done? The horses were still nervous. If they reared up on that loose stuff and lost their footing, they might fall into the chasm, and take the rest of the party with them.

Brock turned to Else. "You know this mountain, girl. Maybe you know of another way down?"

Else shook her head. Then she said, "There's a way my father told me. I never seen it. It'd mean going back. Back up *there*."

"Oh, no," said Flegel. "No, no. Back into that beast's hunting runs? No!"

"Be quiet, Flegel!"

Else went on. "You go across the high pasture and on up a path which winds through the crags. There's a lake up there, he told me, very high. And beyond the lake more crags, and a gap in the crags, and a way down to the glacier. And on the far side of the glacier there's a path leading down the mountain. But we can't go that way. You'd never get your horses over the crags. Anyway, no one goes that way now. Because of the dragon. It nests up there somewhere."

Brock looked at the sky, considering. Above him the mountain was tugging fresh shawls of cloud around its summits. Curtains of rain or snow blurred the distances. The only sounds were the small rattlings and chitterings of stones bounding down the slope as the landslide went on settling.

"We'll try this way," he said at last.

"We could leave the horses behind," ventured Flegel.

"We're not leaving more good horses for that worm," said Brock, swinging himself down from Flegel's mount and starting to lead it up the rockfall. "With the horses under us we still have a hope of being safe back at Knochen by dusk. Leave them behind and we'll be caught on the mountain when night comes down again. Is that what you want?"

Of course it wasn't. Who'd want to be in that place in the dark, thinking each night noise the approaching dragon? Flegel scrambled down off Brezel, and Ansel took the reins from him and started to follow Brock up the fresh scree, coaxing the nervous pony after him. Stones scattered downhill past him, dislodged by Brock's boots and the hooves of the horse. A big rock rattled down, missing Ansel by only a hand's breadth. His own feet were sliding on the loose shale, too, trying to carry him back down between each step. Brezel whickered and tossed his head, jerking his reins and almost pulling Ansel over. Behind him, Flegel and Else were starting to climb, looking up at him nervously each time a larger stone went trundling past them. Flegel kept up a steady murmur of complaint. "Why did I let him lead me up here? Men are like dogs, that's why; there are those that lead and those that follow, and he is one of those who leads, and I am one of those who follow. . ."

The slope grew steeper. The going was achingly slow, but at last Brock was almost at the top; he would be rounding the big rock soon, and starting down to the path on the far side. Ansel's boots sank deep into wet soil, squeezing up water. He heard his master slip and curse up above him and stepped aside just in time as a big, jagged boulder came slithering down the slope, dislodging scores of smaller stones as it went past. He calmed Brezel and stumbled on, trying not to think about the chasm behind him. Instead, he wondered how they would be received in the village when they let it be known they had not killed the dragon. Or maybe Brock would keep quiet about that. Maybe he'd flaunt that old corkindrille skull as he'd planned, and tell them he had slain their worm, and let them work out for themselves that they'd been cheated when he was safe and far away. Else had no reason to like the villagers, so she might go along with the lie. Maybe

Brock would let Else and her mother travel with him. Maybe they could all go away somewhere; somewhere with no mountains and no dragons. . .

Something large and dark came sliding silently down the scree slope. Ansel leapt aside again, and realized as he tugged Brezel after him that it was only a shadow.

But a shadow of what?

Brezel reared up suddenly, snorting in fear, dragging his reins out of Ansel's hand.

"It's come!" screamed Else.

The dragon soared over them. Ansel could hear the wind hissing through the long feathers that spread like fingers from the edges of its wings. Its lizard head glared down at him, letting out a long cry, and echoes kicked back from all the rock faces, as if there were a dozen dragons all crying out in turn. The noise stripped all the thoughts out of Ansel's head and panicked him into a flailing sort of run. He scrambled and struggled uphill, but he went nowhere, for the scree was slithering downhill as fast as he could run up it. Brezel went past him, wading against the stone tide. Ahead, Brock was battling to control Flegel's panicked horse, which was bucking and plunging, dislodging huge sections of the slope.

Ansel screamed silently. The speed of the shifting ground was increasing. He was running as fast as he could, but he was still being carried backwards, downhill, towards the place where the ground ended and there was only a long drop to the river and its jaggedy rocks.

Beside him, with a long groan, the giant rock that had barred their way started to shift. It came at him diagonally across the scree-face, a storm of lesser stones racketing ahead of it like small, grey, scampering animals. He saw Else throw herself out of its way, scrabbling crabwise across the slope. Everything was moving now, earth and stones and rocks and roots all rushing like water downhill towards the lip of the chasm. Overhead the worm soared, confused by the sliding ground, trying to decide which of those struggling shapes it should dive on.

Flegel's horse came crashing sideways down the scree towards Ansel, baring its big teeth, yawning in terror. It was almost on top of him when a bounding rock knocked its feet from under it. Ansel heard the sharp snaps of its cannon bones breaking, and the dreadful shrill neighing as it went under, pummelled and pounded in the surf of stones. He ran on the spot, clawing over the rocks as they rumbled beneath him, watching the big one slew slowly towards him. Above it somewhere was Brock, capering like a carnival clown to keep his balance. Above *him* the whole mountainside seemed to be stirring and shifting as more boulders started to slide. And above the mountainside the dragon wheeled, but Ansel had lost sight of it, and had no time to look for it, for the big rock was rushing at him. At the last instant he flung himself sideways out of its path. He landed on wet earth beyond the landslide's edge, and lay there face down, listening to the stone crushing smaller stones beneath its bulk as it went past him, and then the sudden silence as it tipped over the chasm's edge. A heartbeat later he could hear it again, booming and shattering its way down towards the river far below.

He turned to look for Brezel. He could not see the pony. But then he could not see much of anything; a curtain of dust hung over the hillside. Swooping through it came the dragon, cracking its serpent's tail like a striped whip. It saw Ansel sprawling there below it and screeched in triumph. The noise froze him to the earth as it swept down on him. It landed a little way off and came quickly at him over the rocks with its wings and its neck outstretched, its snout badly painted with Snow's dried blood. Then it veered away, screeching. Something had struck it hard on the side of its head.

Else was standing up among the scattered rocks nearby, readying a second stone. Father Flegel, crouching close to her, shouted, "No, girl! You're just making it angry! Let it eat him!" But Else ignored him, and flung the stone anyway. Her aim was deadly. She'd practised stone-throwing when she was smaller, minding her father's goats on the high meadows. Several times she'd driven off wolves that way, and she'd killed one once. Her stone flew true. It bounced off the dragon's nose, and the dragon flinched and yelped, scrabbling backwards over the rocks with its wings held out wide like a cormorant.

For a moment Ansel thought Else's stones were going to drive it off. If it was only used to hunting sheep and goats it might be startled by prey that fought back. Its head weaved from side to side, studying the girl. The black nostrils flexed and snuffled, scenting. Ansel could hear Flegel's tremulous prayers, and he realized with some spare portion of his mind that the noise of sliding rocks had ended. The landslide was over.

"Go away!" screamed Else. "Flap off, worm!" Another stone flew at the dragon, but this time it jerked aside and the stone missed. Again it made the same grim, bubbling growl that Ansel had heard earlier, before it sprang at him outside the cave. Again Ansel felt himself go rigid at the sound, but this time he was not the dragon's prey. It darted at Else and the friar, half flying and half running over the rocks. Else stooped for another stone but Ansel knew she would not have time to throw one. Flegel knew it too. He shoved her and sent her sprawling in the dragon's path. "Take her!" he screamed, as he turned and fled.

To the charging animal Else must have seemed to vanish, falling down behind the rocks. It soared past her, drawn by Flegel's flapping cloak and habit, by the shrill screams he let out as he ran. He twisted his head and looked back over his shoulder and saw it speeding after him. "It was her!" he squealed. "Have mercy! Eat her, not me!"

The friar ran fast, but the dragon was faster. He scrambled up the scree, but the dragon had wings. It soared across the last few feet that separated them. It lunged its bear-trap head forward on that long muscled neck and snatched him off the ground like a thief swiping a fat purse. Flegel let out a bubbling scream. His legs flailed, his red boots running desperately on air as it dragged him awkwardly into the sky. He screamed again, then stopped abruptly. The wingbeats of the dragon echoed away up the valley, fainter and fainter, until there was only silence.

14

"I'm not sure any more that it *is* a dragon," said Brock, some time later.

They had climbed back from the place of the landslide and were looking out across that high valley again, towards the shepherd's cave with its worm-breached wall. They had found an overhanging crag which gave them a faint sense of shelter, but they all knew that if the dragon wanted them it would have no trouble taking them.

"It has only two legs, and breathes no fire, and whoever heard of a dragon with feathers? Perhaps it is a wyvern, or some other, lesser kind of worm."

"Who cares what it is?" Else said tetchily. "All worms are much alike, I'd reckon, when you are inside their bellies, and that is where we're going to end up, isn't it? The next time it comes it will take us."

Brock ignored her. He was studying the mountain, looking up past the rocky crags around the valley to the snow and ice of the heights above. "Where does it make its nest?" he wondered.

Ansel sat trying to stop shaking, and wondered how long it would take Brock to understand that he was not a dragon hunter any more, but a dragon's *prey*. He kept thinking of Father Flegel, and how surprised the friar had looked when the creature's jaws clamped round him. And Brezel, who had simply vanished, probably carried away down that slow river of stones. Poor Brezel! Ansel felt that he could have saved him somehow, or at least tried to save him. He should have done *something*. . .

They were a miserable sight, the three of them. The horses were gone, and so was their road home. When the dust of the landslide settled they had seen how the track they had hoped to travel down had been swept away: only sections of it remained, interspersed with deep fissures where whole sections of the cliff face had collapsed. Among the rubble they had found the smashed body of Flegel's horse, and had retrieved the rope and a few blankets and one of its saddlebags. Otherwise they had only the clothes they sat in.

Brock said, "Well, we won't be going back down by Knochen, that's for sure. The landslide has seen to that. We must go higher before we go down. That is what God wants of us. No doubt that is why he spared me at the landslide, and let the worm take poor Flegel, who was so full of doubts. . . If we're to get off this mountain we'll have to take the path you spoke of, Else."

The girl was pressed tight against the rock wall they sat beneath, shivering faintly, watching the after-image of the dragon which had not yet faded from her eyes. Her hands kept kneading the fabric of her dress into tight bunches, smoothing it out and then kneading it again. But she felt Brock's eyes on her, and looked at him, and saw his smile. It seemed to warm her a little.

"Your father's path," he said. "The other way down. How do we find it?"

She pointed across the valley to the crags. "Up there," she said.

Her finger wavered and trembled. It took them all a moment to make out the steep, raked ledge that crept up across the cliffs and screes, like a crack on a wall.

"But we can't go that way," she said. "Because of the dragon. . ."

"I will defend us from the dragon," said Brock. "Do you think God would let it harm you? Have faith. He has brought me here to kill it." He smiled at Else and Ansel, touched by the way they watched him, the faint looks of hope on their wan young faces. They made him feel strong, and proud of his strength. He was their protector. He was the one they looked to to lead and defend them.

He sniffed, and gripped his sword's hilt, and looked at the sky. "When it comes again I'll be ready. I'll kill it, and we'll walk down the pass to the town and show its head to the landgrave and the people there."

He set off across the valley, leaving Else and Ansel to follow, lugging the blankets and the one remaining bag.

When the King of France sent his chamberlain to

scale a high mountain, he let him take along three holy men, a carpenter and the royal ladder man, with ladders to lash to its hard-faced crags, and wood and ropes and pins. When Johannes Brock set off up the Drachenberg he had only one young girl and one still younger boy. They took no scaling-ladders, and barely food enough for one lean meal. And King Charles's man had made his climb in summertime, in good weather, not in that day's dim, brownish light, which kept dying into darkness as clouds blew over the crags.

This is madness, thought Ansel, pulling and heaving and tugging and levering himself up the steep way between the rocks, feeling like a beetle on a wall. *This is madness*, he thought again, searching for his way in the blind whiteness of a snow shower and seeing nothing but a confusion of grey shadows, with the shadows of Brock and the girl creeping on through the midst of it. When Else looked back at him her face was white as whey, and he knew that his must look the same. White and weary with the unending fear of that unending day.

It *was* madness. Mountains weren't meant to be climbed. But what else could they do? There was no way down on that side of the Drachenberg. They had to reach the other. They had nowhere to go but up. So they ploughed on, grazed and aching, chilled through, shuddering, making their way out on to impassable ledges and edging back, creeping like rats up impossible chimneys, hands freezing, toes freezing, hearts freezing. And the snow-dusted world unfolded in white and black below them as they rose.

In places the path died away entirely, and they had to make their own way up pocked black slopes of steeply sloping rock, finding their way from foothold to foothold. Before they attempted the first of those, Else said that they must rope themselves together. "That's what the men do if they have to come up this way, looking for strayed sheep. Then if one falls the others can take his weight, and pull him up to safety."

Brock ordered Ansel to fetch out the coil of rope they had been given by the villagers. They each looped it around their chests and knotted it as best they could with their numb fingers, and when they crept onward up the rock the rope stretched between them. Ansel doubted it would do much good – he couldn't see himself and Else being able to haul Brock back up if he fell – but it was good to feel the rope tugging and tautening as the others made their own way up the rock above him. It helped him to believe that he was not quite alone when the next snow shower came swirling off the mountain.

He stopped when the snow closed in, and Else stopped above him. They clung to the cliff and tried to shelter, turning slowly into snowmen as the flakes crusted on their clothes and hair. But after a few moments the rope jerked taught and they were forced to start climbing again. Ansel's fingers grew numb groping for handholds on the freezing rock, and then began to burn with a mysterious, agonizing heat. The wind teased streamers of snot from his cold nose. "Come on!" shouted Brock's voice, bellowing down at him from high above. "If the worm finds us on this cliff it will have us like three eggs in a basket."

Ansel looked up at Else through the slackening snow. She said nothing, but she made a quirking movement with those black, black brows of hers, and he knew she agreed with Brock. He let her go ahead, and climbed after her. She was slower than him, so sometimes his face was on a level with her feet and he could see the way her felt boots were starting to come apart, baring her bloody, blistered heels. He knew she must be in pain, but she did not speak of it, and he thought that was brave of her.

But Brock kept climbing, tireless. He could picture the dragon's lair somewhere above him, a cave in a crag, the rocks around it scattered with bones and droppings. Maybe there would be gold in there, like in the old tales. But it wasn't the thought of the gold that pulled Brock up the mountain. It was the worm itself, and the chance it offered him of turning all his lies into one startling truth. *Brock the worm killer*, he thought. *Johannes Von Brock, the dragon slayer. . .*

The wind howled and hooed, trying out unnerving dragon noises. It was cold enough to crack rocks, thought Else, struggling along behind the armoured man. Maybe the breath of dragons wasn't fire at all, but searing ice. And maybe this was how the dragon caught its prey, by luring men like Brock so high that they were too weary and weak to fight it when it found them.

They were halfway up another blank-faced cliff when the snow returned. This squall was even heavier than the last, the feathering flakes blotting out everything. Even Brock was forced to stop, and Ansel clung miserably to the rock face, chilled through and shivering, fearing that at any moment his dizziness and his frozen fingers would conspire to make him topple off. Sometimes the wind slackened, and he could hear Else weeping with cold and weariness above him.

At last even Brock had to admit that they needed a place to hide and rest. They came to a hole that ice and water had scooped out of the mountain's side, and they crept into it. It was as cold as a tomb in there, but it was warmer than being outside in the wind. They sat side by side, like birds on a branch. They pushed close to each other, each hoping that the others might be warmer. The snow had stopped, but the sky was quickly growing dim. While they'd been climbing the short day had spent itself. Sexton-black, the night buried them.

"What if the dragon comes again?" asked Else.

"The worm hunts by daylight," Brock said. He was as bruised and shaken by the climb as either of the children, but he knew that he must not let them see it. They were depending on him. Besides, he told himself, they were still alive, weren't they, the three of them. Just as poor Flegel would be, if only the friar had listened to him. He had the measure of the dragon now.

"A beast that hunts by day won't hunt in the dark," he said. "It'll be snug in its nest somewhere. We're safe enough till morning." He tipped his head back against the stony wall and was soon asleep, leaving Else and Ansel to listen to his snores and think about all the other beasts they knew of, like cats and spiders, owls and wolves, which were quite as happy to hunt by day as by night.

"What do you think it will feel like?" asked Else, just as Ansel was drifting into sleep himself. "When it eats us? Will it hurt? Will we die quick, or will we be alive still when we go down its throat?"

Ansel couldn't answer her, of course. He snuggled a bit closer to her, and that seemed to satisfy her. A little later he heard her breathing slow, and thought, *She's asleep*, and wondered if he should try to stay awake, to watch and listen for the dragon. But almost before the thought was formed he was asleep himself. Exhausted by the cold and the climbing, he slept so deeply that he would not have noticed if the dragon had fluttered down to perch beside him. It wasn't like real sleep at all. It was as if tiredness had battered him senseless.

15

Ansel awoke in light. The sun had risen over a bony knob of the mountain and was shining into his face. He remembered where he was, and why. He scrambled up, but there was no sign of the dragon. He was surprised at how high they had climbed. The valley lay far below him. It was still night down there. Day began a few feet below his perch, above the shadow of that eastern spur, which stretched along the crags like a tidemark.

He looked up. Above him, the narrow path they'd tried to follow spidered up between big rocks and vanished over a sort of shelf. Above that, the sky was blue as Mary's robe, and blessedly empty of dragons. There was a rushing noise. He'd heard it in the night, but then he had thought it was just the wind. Now there was no wind, and he could see that the sound was made by a white cataract that plunged down the mountainside not far from the crack they had sheltered in. It threw out a cloud of spray, and the sun shone through the spray and made a rainbow. It looked like a promise from God.

Else stirred and moaned. Brock's armour grated as he tried to work a cramp out of his leg. Ansel squirrelled in the saddlebag and found them breakfast: stale bread, dry mutton, a slurp of bitter wine washed down with water from a nearby rill. He wished that he could show them his rainbow, but the sun was climbing fast and it had already faded.

"Up," said Brock. The rising sun was warming his armour, and he seemed to draw strength from it. He started up the path, not waiting for Ansel and Else.

The worst of the climb was behind them. The

path went up in three last steep zigzags, then led them over a crag's brow on to a broad snowfield. Black outcroppings of rock jabbed up through the snow, and in the rocks' lee, where the snow had not laid, brownish grass rustled in the breeze. Despite the snow the air was warm and the sun beat upon the whiteness of the snow, which shone its warmth back at them, until Else loosened her sheepskin shawl and Ansel pulled his mittens off. His numbed fingers burned as the feeling started coming back to them.

The ground sloped upwards to a broad-backed ridge. They reached its top, and looked down into a bowl of rocks where a grey lake lay. Along the shore the lake water had frozen in big, rippled, whitish plates. Further out, patches of open water were being ruffled into wavelets by the rising wind. No reeds fringed that lake; no lilies lay on it; no birds sang over it. Beyond it, the mountain went up again, an arc of rock and snow, a blinding white summit hanging high above. Clouds were brewing behind the mountain, but otherwise the sky was empty, innocent. Maybe the dragon was hunting on the other side of the mountains that morning. Maybe it was sleeping off its feasts of the day before.

"More bad weather's coming," said Else, turning her face to the sun, making the most of the warmth, which she knew would not last. Brock watched her with a curious expression. His eyes kept darting to the heights of the mountain.

They untied themselves from one another, cutting the tight, sodden knots which they numbed fingers could not undo. Ansel tied the lengths of rope together and coiled them round him as they started on.

It took several hours for them to make their way around the lake to the crags on the far side. There they picked up the path which Else's father had told her of. Faint and faded, it dropped giddily down slopes of scree and shale into a steep-sided valley. Spiky crags crowned with starved-looking clumps of pine thrust out into the valley, and at their feet lay the glacier. Ansel had not quite believed in it when Else and Brock talked about it – a river of ice, creeping forever down the mountain. Yet there it was, vast and cold, hatched all over with crevices and chasms, and though he could not see it moving he could *hear* it: the faint grinding and grumbling as it dragged its way over the rocks, and sometimes a crisp icy crack from the fractured surface.

Beyond it, on the valley's far wall, a snowy track showed white across the face of a steep black cliff.

"That's the path," said Else.

"Good," said Brock. "But we are not going down yet."

Ansel looked at his master. Brock seemed barely to have noticed the terrible way down, or the enticing glimpse of the path at the bottom of it. He had turned his back on it, and he was studying the crags and spires of the mountain above them as if it were a castle, and he was planning to storm it.

"What do you mean, sir?" asked Else.

"I mean that I have a dragon to fight."

His words faded into the wind and the sunlight. Else didn't speak, and Ansel couldn't. They looked at each other, and Ansel shook his head a little to show that he didn't know what Brock meant either.

"It must be up there, somewhere," said Brock. "Up in all that snow and stone. Its nest. Its eyrie. But how do we call it down?"

Again the wind took his words away, across the valley. Again Ansel and Else exchanged a look. This time, Else ventured to question what Brock had said. "We don't want to call it down, sir," she said. "We want it stay up there till we're far away."

"No," said Brock. He smiled at her. His eyes had a wild shine to them. "No. Don't you see? That's why we've come here. The other path was shut to us, so we had to climb up here, close to its lair. So that I can kill it. It's fate. God's hand. Call it what you like. I'm not starting down until that worm is dead. I'll take its head. That should be proof enough. . ." He switched his gaze back to the mountain. "I thought we might climb up to its lair, but it may be beyond the reach of any man. Those towering cliffs. . ."

Ansel felt the same way he had the previous day, when he saw that the landslide had swept their path away. He'd thought Brock strong and hard as a mountain. Now it seemed something had shifted inside the dragon hunter. He had toppled into one of his own stories.

"Why just the head?" Brock asked himself. "I'll take its whole carcass down the mountain with me. It's a flying beast, so it must be light, like a bird. I expect there are learned men who would pay me well for the hide and bones of such a prodigy. . . Damnation, perhaps I'll set up as a learned man myself. I'll boil its bones and dry its skin and set it up on a cart. It'll be the talk of every town from here to the sea!" He turned showman suddenly, pulling his leather cap off, bowing to a pair of ravens which were circling above a nearby crag. "*Observe, My Lords and Ladies, a Survivor from the*

World before the Flood. Johannes Von Brock's Great Worm, the only genuine Dragon ever seen. (Or wyvern. Or whatever it be.)" He saw Ansel staring at him, and reached down to ruffle his hair. "What? Surely you don't want to go home without a prize?"

Ansel wondered if the cold which had got inside his fingers and made them numb and clumsy had done something similar to his master's brains. Brock seemed to go straight from wanting a thing to believing he could have it. Had he forgotten the dragon's jaws and its claws? Had he forgotten how easily it had torn up his horse and wolfed down his comrade? Had he forgotten that this was the dragon's mountain, not his? Ansel didn't want a prize to take back to the lowlands. He'd be happy just to get down with his life.

But Brock wanted the worm, and Brock had a plan. He'd been turning it over in his mind all morning, while they crept along that lake shore, slowed down by Else with her torn boots and bloody feet. At first she had angered him. He had wished that Flegel was still with them, so that the friar could explain to him why God had chosen to lumber His champion with a lame girl. But then, as if God himself had leaned down out of Heaven and whispered it in his ear, he understood.

Else saw the greedy way that he was looking at her. She tried on a smile, in the hope that it would please him, but he just kept staring. She edged backwards, retreating from him the same way she would from a dog she wasn't sure of. "What, sir?" she asked. "What is it?"

Brock caught her wrist in his gauntleted hand to stop her going any further. "Rope!" he said. He said it to Ansel, though Ansel didn't understand and he had to say it again. "The rope, boy, or have you turned deaf as well as dumb?"

Ansel shrugged himself out of the coiled rope and passed it to Brock, who took it with his free hand.

"Don't!" said Else, straining away from him.

"Don't wriggle so, girl," said Brock.

Else looked past him at Ansel. "Make him stop!"

Ansel hesitated, torn between pity for her and loyalty to his master.

"He's gone mad," she said. "Can't you see? Men lose their wits on the heights sometimes. The thin air addles them."

"Don't heed her, Ansel," Brock warned. "I know what I'm about. I'm here to slay this beast, remember. Trust me, boy. All's well. No hurt shall come to Else. You have my word on it. . ."

He quickly looped the rope's end round her wrists and started to knot them. Ansel wanted to tell him to stop, but the words faded away, as usual, before he could wrestle them out of his mouth. He ran forward instead, and tugged on Brock's cloak.

Brock shoved him aside. "Leave me alone, Ansel. Don't you see? Those peasants had it right. They left her up here as bait. Like St George's princess. That part of the story must be true, too. That's how you lure these beasts. Like tethering a lamb to lure a wolf. Except to lure our worm we must offer it a choicer morsel. A good, wriggling Christian maid. It is evil, you see, and it cannot resist her innocence."

"*No! You can't!*" Ansel shouted, but he shouted it inside himself, and of course Brock couldn't hear.

"No, no, no, no!" Else was saying. Her eyes showed white all round, like Snow's had when the dragon got her. When Brock took no heed of her she started screaming. "No! No!"

Brock laughed. "That's right, girl!" he said. "Scream! Scream, Else! Let the worm hear you!"

He looked at the sky, scanning it quickly for approaching wings. Nothing. Else, afraid now to cry out again or even speak, fell on her knees in the snow. Brock lifted her upright again. "You will be all right!" he told her. "I promise you. I don't mean to sacrifice you to this beast, like your heathen neighbours tried to. You are bait, that's all. This time, I will be ready for it when it comes. I shall kill it before it can harm you."

Talking steadily to her, he coaxed the roped girl uphill to a broad slope of clear snow between two rock towers. There he tied the end of her halter tight around a snag of stone and retired to the shelter of those tall rocks to watch and wait.

16

Ansel didn't know what to do. He wanted to run and unhitch Else; snick the rope with his knife and free her. Brock might be his master, but when he looked at Else, grizzling at the end of that leash, waiting for the dragon to drop on her, he knew he couldn't let Brock use her like that. She made him think again of poor Brezel. He had to save her. He fidgeted, turning this way and that as he wondered what to do.

"Keep still!" hissed Brock. He sat in a nook of the rocks with his sword stuck upright in the ground in front of him. He said, "If you wriggle more than Else the worm might take you instead. Is that what you want?" He looked away from the tethered girl for a moment, staring deep into Ansel's eyes. He could see Ansel's small thoughts in them as plain as tadpoles in a pair of puddles. "Ansel, it will be all right."

His attention went back to the girl, and the crags beyond the girl, and the empty sky. Ansel sat still, wishing he had a voice, so that he might try and make Brock see how wrong he was. But as he sat there he started to realize that sitting still might be the best thing he could do. Here among the rocks Brock had finally found shelter from the wind. The sunlight was hazy, but there was still warmth in it. The rocks soaked it up, and they grew warm too. Brock, in his skin of tin, must have been warmer still. He stared past his sword at Else, who had sunk to her knees out there on the rope's end, silent under the merciless sky.

"You need not fear for her, Ansel," said Brock. "I'll not let it take her. I'm ready this time. Always before it's had the advantage of us. At the cave yesterday I was too startled to think. I was scared, I admit. It stunned me. That's how it took poor old Snow. And when it dropped on us at the landslide, I couldn't get close enough to fight it. But I'm close enough now, and I'm not scared any more. All I need do is watch. And you'll watch with me. You're a brave lad. I might need your help, come the time."

Brock watched. Ansel watched. The wind ruffled the grass. No wings shadowed the cliffs. It was almost possible to think that yesterday had been a dream and there were no such things as dragons, after all.

After a while Brock's head dipped. He caught himself, frowned, blinked, ran his eyes round the rims of the sky. Else flopped on the snow, beaten but uneaten. Clouds darkened the air behind the mountain, but Brock's hide baked in sunshine. His head dipped again, and then again, and the next time he did not lift it.

A minute more, and Ansel heard a soft snore. He made himself stay where he was till he was sure. Brock was asleep. Brock was deeply asleep, worn out by the scrambling and clambering of the previous day. Ansel envied him. He was tired too, but fear kept him awake. He let the hunter snore, snore, snore, then carefully, silently he slipped from his perch and edged past Brock and tiptoed away, following the rope across the snow to Else.

She looked up when he reached her. She didn't look as grateful as he'd imagined she would. Maybe she was wondering why he had waited so long. He tugged his knife out and began sawing at the rope.

"Quickly!" she whispered.

Ansel smiled to show her it was all right, and nodded at Brock, to make her see the dragon hunter was asleep.

"I don't care about him! What about the dragon?"

The rope parted. She stumbled up, holding out her hands for Ansel to cut the knot that still tied them together. Just then, a shadow fell over them.

It's come for us! thought Ansel. *This is our punishment for doubting Brock.*

But when he looked up, there was no dragon there. Just a scarf of black cloud, spilling off the mountain. A cold wind came ahead of it, driving white foam across the lake. Already the cliff where Brock believed the creature laired was smudged out by curtains of snow.

"Brock will wake!" said Else. When Ansel had freed her hands she turned and ran, and he ran with her. Their feet rasped and crunched and squeaked in the thick snow. When Ansel looked back to see if Brock was following, he saw – nothing at all. The rocks, the mountainside, the armoured man, all were hidden by a deep whiteness. He started shoving Else towards shelter.

"No!" she told him. "He will find us there! We must go down!"

Ansel thought about the downward path. The screes and then the boulders and then the cliffs of ice. He would rather have faced the dragon. But fear of Brock's madness kept him running, stumbling along beside Else towards the top of the screes. The snowstorm broke around them. Snowflakes whirled up, down, sideways, furring their sleeves and mittens. Else stopped to tug her fleece-cloak tighter. She shouted at Ansel over the sudden rush of the wind.

"Brave as a hero, you were. You could've run, but you stopped and saved me."

Ansel, in spite of everything, grinned. He knew he wasn't all that brave. Not brave enough to go away and have to live with the memory of leaving her as dragon-bait. It had been just selfishness, really, that made him saw that rope through. He was glad of her thanks, though. It made him feel a bit less bad about betraying Brock.

Else kissed him in the middle of his snow-wet forehead, the way a mother might, or a big sister at least. Then, taking their best guess at the way, they set off together blindly down the steepening slope.

Brock woke in the snow with a shout no one heard. He had been dreaming, but now he was awake he could not remember what the dream had been about. There was a sour taste in his mouth.

He looked for Ansel and found him gone. He found his way to the rock he'd tied the girl to. The rope was still knotted round it, stretching away from him into the vortex of the snow, but when he tugged at it there was no Else on the other end. He reeled it in and stared at the frayed end. Bitten off? Had the dragon taken his bait while he slept, like a fish outwitting a dozy angler?

No, not the dragon, he realized. The boy. Ansel. He felt something that was part anger but mostly pity, because surely God would not let the boy live long now that he had broken faith with His champion. "Ansel!" he bellowed into the blizzard. "Else!"

No reply, only the mad wailing of the wind. What a fool he'd been, letting himself sleep! It was the air up here. It wasn't thick enough for a man to breathe. He groped for his sword, sheathed it, and wound the long rope quickly around his body, knotting it there in case he needed it for his descent. By God, this snow had come on quickly! Every direction looked the same now. Whichever way he turned there was nothing but a rushing whiteness.

He cupped his hands round his mouth. "Ansel! Where are you?" he shouted, and then remembered that the boy couldn't answer.

"Else?"

Something seemed to lurch and move, behind the snow. It wouldn't be hunting in this blizzard, would it? Jesu, was that only a dragonish crag crouched there in the whiteness? Or was it a craggy dragon?

"Ansel!" he bellowed. "To me!"

The snow spun around him. He stumbled in a deep drift and fell, floundering. When he raised himself up the dragon was a few feet off, watching him.

Down, down, down. The first part of the scree slope lay in the ridge's lee, sparing them the worst of the wind and the snow, but they had no more idea of where the thin path ran than if they had been stumbling blindfold down it in the midnight dark. The stones of the slope were frozen into one cold mass, and perhaps that saved them. Down, down, down they went, and dislodged no more than a handful of pebbles and small boulders, which vanished into the whiteness ahead without any sound that Ansel ever heard.

Else kept shouting things, quite close to his ear, but he couldn't hear her either.

Further down the slope the snow lay thicker, drifted over large boulders and small outcroppings of rock. It became hard to tell whether they were going up or down. Ansel fell and dropped the saddlebag he had been carrying, and could not find it again. Then boulders began to emerge out of the whiteness all around them, like grease spots soaking into linen. They blundered into the faint shelter of a barn-sized stone whose surface was carved with swerving, fluted lines, like the grain of wood. There they slapped and shook the matted snow off their clothes, shuddered, clapped their chilled hands, hugged each other for warmth. The wind snarled. The snow rushed past horizontally, giving Ansel the giddy feeling that he was still moving.

"He's mad!" Else shouted. "Your master's mad!

The mountains work that way on some men. The mountain and the dragon between them have driven him stark mad. He's worse than that lot at Knochen."

A little later she yelled, "Do you think he'll find us?"

Eventually the storm began to falter. The wind lost interest in them and went roaring off to trouble some other mountain. A few last snowflakes dithered down like exhausted moths. A cold light filled the valley. The sun showed briefly, like a white coin, heatless and colourless behind the speeding clouds. Little by little, Ansel and Else began to see their surroundings.

They were not where Ansel had thought. In the blizzard, he had imagined that they were running straight down the scree slope, and that they had come to rest among the band of giant boulders at its foot. But it was not so. They had blundered diagonally across the slope instead, and had found their way out on to one of those narrow, rocky promontories which overlooked the glacier. At its end, thirty feet from Ansel and Else, four weathered pine trees stood. The fresh snow slid in heavy packets from their branches and dropped on the ground with weary hushing sounds. Just below them a tall, upright slab of rock sheltered a small ledge which had stayed almost free of snow. Something on that ledge caught the light.

"Is that Brock?" asked Else, flinching back as if she'd glimpsed the dragon itself.

Ansel shook his head. It was not a man, laid there on that lonely rock. Was it only ice, or some shining stone? But there seemed to be more than one. Yes. . . As the storm swept away towards the lowlands and the sky above him lightened, he could see dozens of gleaming things there.

His curiosity made him forget for a moment his cold-seared hands and toes and the ankle he had twisted coming down the screes. He set off along the promontory, limping a little, squinting against the dazzle as the sun peeked through the thinning clouds and rebounded blindingly from the snow-covered glacier below.

"Ansel! Be careful!" shouted Else.

Echoes boomed along the mountainsides. Half a mile away, a dollop of snow as big as a tithe-barn detached itself from a cliff and went rumbling and smouldering down into the valley. Else looked back, a hand to her mouth. Ansel scurried on. He pushed between the pines, over a brown lawn of fallen needles and down a mossy cleft between two rocks. It let him out on to the shelf he had seen from higher up. As he stepped out of the cleft he dislodged something which fell with a clang. It was the breastplate from a soldier's armour, rusted to the same colour as the pine needles, its straps rotted away. He stared down at it, and then around at the other objects which lay all about him, scattered there in the thin snow.

A lady's mirror.

The blade of a halberd.

A string of jewels.

The fittings from a bridle.

A scrap of sodden yellow fabric.

More bits of armour, some rustier than others, some still shining dully.

Bright stones; small heaps of quartz, like dirty snow, with veins of glinting gold.

One of Father Flegel's raspberry leather boots.

Ansel stared at that boot. It seemed to have fallen out of another world. He did not understand, for a moment, how the boot had come here.

And then he did.

I am in the dragon's lair, he thought. Brock had been wrong. The creature did not live on the heights of the mountain. They were too cold and high and spiny for even a dragon to make its home on. It nested *here*.

He started walking carefully backwards towards the crack that he had emerged from. All around him now, among the litter of bright, shining things, he saw bones. He'd not noticed them at first, for most were as greeny-grey and lichenous as the rocks they lay among. Bones of cattle, bones of sheep, bones of human beings, the bones of Else's father, maybe. A man's finger bone with a scuffed iron ring still in place. A small skull which rolled a little way with a hollow trundling sound when Ansel caught it with his heel.

And among the bones, more bright things. Round and yellow like October birch leaves. Coins. Gold coins.

Ansel stopped moving. He stood frozen, terrified that the dragon might return at any moment, but snared by the glint of the coins. The dragon must have been drawn by them too. Magpie-like, it had gathered all these shining things and brought them to this high ledge. The coins lay in a heap, mixed with rusty iron bands and hinges and a lock, the remains of a strongbox that had long since rotted away. Perhaps those fittings had been polished to a high sheen when the box was new. Perhaps that was what had made the dragon take it, not knowing or caring how much money was inside.

How long would it take a thick oak box to rot away to nothing? Ansel wondered. How long had the dragon haunted this place, heaping up its treasures? And why?

He stooped, and was about to start scooping the coins into his pockets, when he heard the flap of its big wings directly overhead.

He crushed himself back into the cleft between the rocks as it came down, landing not ten feet away. It perched at the edge of the ledge, its back towards Ansel, looking out over the glacier. Too scared to move or breathe, Ansel huddled in his hiding place and watched it, mesmerized by the cat-like to-and-fro twitching of the tip of its striped tail.

It folded its wings like two awnings. It turned towards him, and he thought his heart would stop, sure that it had sensed or scented him. But it was intent on its collection. It had a shiny new find to add to it. It put the thing down and hopped fussily around, nudging its treasures carefully into new positions with delicate touches of its snout. This latest prize was shinier than all its other trinkets, and had to be put in pride of place, where the sun could glint on it to best advantage.

The dragon was so busy that it was a while before Ansel was able to see what its new trophy was. Then, finally satisfied, it moved away towards the edge of the ledge again, and he could see what it had been doing.

On top of a scraped-together heap of quartz and metal lay Brock's sword.

17

Else was starting to follow Ansel towards the pines when the dragon came. She caught the flash of its wings out of the corner of her eye, bright as a carnival flag against the hanging fields of snow. She was down in the snow in a heartbeat, tugging the dirty fleece over herself as best she could, trying to hide her tattered finery.

It didn't see her. Maybe it wasn't looking for prey. It carried something in its jaws which shone, flicking a bright spark of light into Else's eyes as it dropped out of sight behind the pines. She knew it had gone down on to the ledge. Had Ansel seen it coming? Had he escaped in time? She hadn't any way of knowing.

If he had been anyone else, and the dragon had caught him, she would have heard him scream, but she didn't think that Ansel would break his eerie silence even for the dragon. She envisioned him being gobbled up, soundless and uncomplaining. It brought tears into her eyes. She blinked them away.

"There is nothing I can do, is there?" she said aloud, but very, very quietly. "It's got him or it hasn't. Poor little scrap. There's nothing I can do."

She waited, watching, hoping to see Ansel come haring back between the pines. "What did he have to go down there for? Stupid! Stupid!" She wanted to save him. She wanted to scramble down on to the ledge and save him if the dragon had him. But she was a sensible girl. She knew the difference between real life and stories, and she knew that bravery like that would only end up with both of them in the dragon's belly. And even more than she wanted to help Ansel, she wanted to live. She edged away backwards over the snow, thinking, *Poor little scrap.*

The dragon lifted up its head and sang to the brightening sky. Deep rumbling notes like a bass viol, rising to a shrill screech. It spread out its wings. It lashed its tail. It loosed a series of short, piercing notes like crossbow bolts, and the sound of its song rebounded from the mountains, and set off rumbling falls of snow on the steeps above the glacier.

Ansel covered his ears and watched. The hilt of Brock's sword shone among the dragon's tarnished treasures like a cross of gold.

So was Brock dead? Had it found him and eaten him? Ansel could not think how else it would have come by his sword. He thought, *If it killed Brock, it will kill me and Else; there will be no one to stop it.* And he thought, *If I had not cut her free, Brock might have slain it. His plan might have worked. Now he's dead, and I'm stuck in this crack, and the dragon will eat me. . .*

The dragon kept singing. It made strange little hopping movements with its wings stretched wide. It was like a dance, thought Ansel. He remembered watching birds dance like that, out in the water meads with his mother when he was little. How they'd laughed together at the silly waterfowl, in springtime. The he-birds had bobbed their heads about and minced around each other on their spindly legs. They'd fanned out their tail feathers like hands of cards, and aimed their beaks at the sky. "They are showing off to the hen-birds," Ansel's mother had told him. "That's their way of saying, 'Look at me! So proud! So handsome! I'll make you a good husband, little hen!'"

The dragon filled its lungs and shrilled its song again. It turned right round, holding out its wings, lifting its feather-fringed tail like a flag. It cocked its head towards the mountains, watching the sky.

It is waiting for a mate, Ansel realized. *It is waiting for another dragon to come. It wants to build a nest, and raise a brood of little dragonlets.*

And for a moment, just for a moment, he was not scared of the creature any more. He felt sorry for it. He understood something of its dreadful loneliness. For how many springtimes had it been carrying shiny things up here to decorate its lair, and bellowing its mating cry into the empty sky? How far had it flown, and over how many mountains, searching for another of its kind? And not finding one. Not ever hearing an answer to its calls, except for echoes bounding back off rock faces and the grumble of avalanches. And years had gone by, and now it was old, and all it wanted was the companionship of another dragon. But maybe there were no others. Maybe the others were all dead.

Suddenly, in the middle of its dance, it stopped, and stiffened. Its head went down, and its posture changed. It had caught a scent. *Another dragon?* thought Ansel, almost hopefully.

But no.

The dragon had scented *him*.

It turned its head and its yellow eye glared at him. It curled its scaly lip and snarled.

Ansel scrambled deeper into the cleft. He shoved himself into a space so tight that he had to twist his shoulders sideways and the two walls of rock clamped his head between them, keeping his face turned towards the dragon.

A rack of ribs crunched under its claws like dry wicker as it prowled across the ledge and stuck its head into the cleft. Its claws scraped on the rocks, trying to prise them apart, as if Ansel were an oyster and the rocks his shell. The cleft filled with its stinking breath. Ansel started to stammer out a prayer, but the dragon roared, putting him off. He wondered if he was in his own tomb. Behind him the cleft widened again, leading up towards the pines, the way he had come. But he wouldn't dare leave by that route. The dragon could flap its wings and be up there in an instant, waiting for him. Even if it grew bored and left him alone, he wouldn't know if it had really gone away; it might be lurking out there, watching for him, like a cat on guard outside a mouse hole.

But it must grow hungry, he promised himself. *Maybe it will fly away, fly right away to find some easier meal. When I hear its wings flapping, then I'll sneak out.*

But how long might that take? It was cold between those rocks. He hadn't realized it when he first pushed his way through the cleft, but the sun never reached there. The rock faces were slick with ice and frozen moss, and Ansel's breath came out as steam. The beast's breath steamed too. It snorted twin plumes of vapour from its nostrils like a fiery dragon in a story. Ansel crammed himself deeper into the cold crevice.

Suddenly something clonged like a cowbell

out on the ledge. The dragon snorted again and straightened, tugging its head free of the cleft to look behind it. A stone fell somewhere, clattering. Then another, clanking this time against a rusted shield. The dragon turned itself around and went prowling out across the ledge.

"Ansel!"

Ansel looked behind him, then up. Else's bundled head stared down at him from the crack of sky at the cleft's top. He thought of her at the landslide, pelting the beast with stones.

The dragon roared.

"Ansel, run!" hissed Else, and the dragon heard her. Ansel saw it spring into the sky, spreading its wings as it went. He heard Else's shriek as it soared over her, and he was running, without meaning to, or knowing that he had even started to move. It was as if his fear was a big hand that was shoving him out of the cleft and across the ledge. Some dead man's ribs got caught around his ankle, making him stumble. He snatched Brock's sword and lugged it after him. Under the sword was an old shield. Flakes of bright paint fell from it when Ansel snatched it up. They swirled around him like a many-coloured blizzard while he shoved his arm through its two leather straps.

One of the straps snapped soggily, rotted through by years of damp, but the other held. Thus armed, he went scrambling back into the cleft and up it towards the pines. Else was wailing somewhere above him. The shadows of the dragon's vast wings flapped across the slice of sky above him. The shield banged heavily against his knees and the sword he dragged behind him scraped and sparked along the rocks.

He came out into daylight. Else was among the pines, where the snow-heavy boughs hung down low to the ground. The dragon kept sticking its head in to get her and then pulling back, alarmed by the heaps of snow which were dropping from the higher branches to burst upon its back. Else scrambled about on all fours in the pine-needle shadows, trying to keep out of its way. She was trying not to make a sound, but screams and whimpers kept bursting out of her, and they made the dragon more eager than ever to reach her.

Ansel scuffed through the snow towards the creature. It didn't know he was there, or maybe didn't care. Its tail snaked past him, feathers flapping, and he had lean backwards to save himself from being knocked flat. He lifted Brock's too-heavy sword in both hands, letting the shield dangle. The dragon darted forward again, rummaging in the dark under the pines for Else. Its tail lay like a snake along a snowy rock. Almost without meaning to, Ansel brought the sword down. It was so heavy it just seemed to fall, taking his hands down with it. He watched it drop. It hit the dragon's tail a few feet from its tip, and cut it almost through.

Blood splashed and spouted, deep red against the whiteness of the snow. The dragon shrieked, and the sound was red too, somehow, a blazing explosion of red inside Ansel's head. He dropped the sword and blundered sideways as the dragon whipped round, roaring in pain and rage. The mountains roared with it, echoes and avalanches booming among the watching crags. Snow crashed off the pines, knocking the dragon sideways, and almost knocking Ansel down too as he struggled away from it. The shield still hung from his arm by its one strap, encumbering him. He tried to shake it off, but the strap was snagged on his clothes, so he dragged it with him like a broken wing, ploughing through deep snow towards the nearest rocks.

Behind him the dragon snarled and

whimpered. The snow around it was scuffed and pink with soaked-in blood. It lifted its tail, but the end hung broken, nearly severed. Spreading its wings, it heaved itself into the air, roaring again at Ansel, but the loss of its tail had lamed it somehow; it slewed sideways and crashed against a tree, dislodging another rush of snow and flushing Else out of the shadows beneath the bottom branches. She scrambled after Ansel to the rocks. Together they pushed through between them, looking for somewhere to hide: a cave, an overhang, even a crack like the one he had just been caught in would be welcome. But there was nothing. Just five boulders perched in a half-circle at the top of a steep slope of snow reaching down to the glacier.

The dragon roared again, not far behind. They saw its lurching shadow on the snow beyond the rocks. Watching it, Else missed her footing and plunged down the slope, rolling downhill through the crumbly snow for twenty feet before she managed to stop herself. The dragon roared. The noise drove an idea into Ansel's head. He held the shield over his head and waded downhill in the wake of scumbled snow that Else had made. He reached her as she stood up, dashing snow from her face. He wrenched the old shield off his arm, snapping the strap, and set it face down on the snow.

She stared at him, and understood. The dragon's angry shadow spilled over them. It stood at the top of the ridge and roared, afraid to come down after them on foot in the deep snow, afraid to fly with its broken tail. It roared, and watched Else and Ansel as they clambered on to the shield. There wasn't room for both of them, not really, but they crammed themselves on somehow, and as Ansel lifted his boots from the snow the shield started to slide.

The dragon saw them start to slither away from him, quickly gathering speed. It started after them, but the snow gave way beneath its weight and it almost fell, whipping its maimed tail up to balance itself and scattering specks of blood like bright red flowers across the slope. It roared again, but Else and Ansel barely heard it. Their ears were filled with the high hiss of the shield as it raced over the snow. It spun around and around as it swept downhill, and spilled them at last, gasping and giddy, into a drift on the surface of the glacier.

The dragon was gone. There was nothing on the rocky promontory behind them but those four pines.

"Where is it?" said Else, craning her neck, the crags swinging dizzily round her.

Ansel looked too. No dragon.

Else sat down, and laid her hand on the shield. "We used to slide down the fields on wooden sledges in Knochen in the wintertime, when I was small," she said, with a sort of wondering sound in her voice, as if the memory was new-found and very strange. She looked up at Ansel, and said, "I thought the dragon had you when I saw it come down. I was going to creep away. I thought I was too frightened to try and fetch you out. I was halfway gone before I realized I wasn't. This isn't a mountain to be left alone on, is it?"

Ansel shook his head and grinned.

The girl tied up her headscarf, which had come undone, spilling her greasy hair across her face. She looked at the crags again, narrowing her eyes suspiciously, as if the rocks were the faces of people she didn't quite trust. "It's gone," she said. "Maybe you killed it. It might have bled to death by now, after that gash you made in its tail. Sliced it like a sausage! It can't fly any more, at least. It'll crawl away somewhere and die. You're the dragon killer, not old Brock."

Ansel shook his head. He thought he'd most

likely only wounded the dragon. He thought he'd probably only made it angry.

He stood up and walked off a little way, wallowing through the deep snow. He had not gone far before a hole opened up in front of him. He peered over its edge, down into the heart of the glacier: a cold glass world of fluted blue ice and frigid shadows. If their makeshift sledge had carried them another few feet they would have plunged into it. His heart beat quickly just looking at it, imagining that plunge. He looked around. All over the surface of the glacier he saw similar gashes and pitfalls, and sinister dips and hollows in the snow where more lay hidden. From high above they'd looked no more than shadows. He'd thought they might sledge all the way on the old shield; now he saw they'd have to walk. And night would soon be drawing on again, and they had no food.

The triumph he'd felt at seeing off the dragon turned sour. It wasn't only the worm that was trying to kill him, it was the mountain as well. And the mountain was worse than the dragon, because the dragon wanted to eat him, but the mountain wanted nothing at all.

But Else seemed almost cheerful. He wondered

if the downhill rush had left her light-headed. She hummed a tune, tearing strips from the hem of her felt dress to hold the remnants of her shoes to her scabbed and frostbitten feet. "We can go down from here," she said. "We can creep our way down the glacier to its snout. There is a lake there, and another below it, and a river going down into the valley."

She stood up, and took his hand, and they started walking, crunching across the snow, slithering over the steep ridges and short, sudden drops which stretched over the surface of the glacier like frozen waves. "We won't go back to Knochen," she said, as she limped along. "Not after how they treated me. We'll send word to my mother, and we'll all go together to the lowlands. She'll take care of you, Ansel, when she hears how you looked after me. Ansel the dragon killer."

She smiled at him, looking hopeful for the first time since he'd known her. She was still smiling when the dragon landed behind them in an explosion of flung snow. It came down heavily and almost fell as it landed, claws skittering on the ice. Else screamed, and on either wall of the valley the snow answered her, white streamers pummelling down between the stark crags. But they were far away, and the dragon ignored them. It ignored Else too, and came stalking through the snow at Ansel, who tried to back away. But a yielding feeling underfoot warned him that he was no longer standing on firm ice but only on a skin of frozen snow which blizzards had spun across the mouth of a crevasse.

He looked down, and took another step back, interested to see what would happen. There was a soft crump from somewhere beneath him as a mass of snow detached itself from the underside of the snow-skin and plummeted into some enormous blue depth.

Else had gone quiet, watching, huddled against the snow twenty feet away, half hidden by the snow which the dragon had scattered as it landed. Ansel knew that she was keeping very still and silent in the hope that it would eat him instead of her, and he did not blame her, because he also knew that if he had been in her place he would have done the selfsame thing. He looked at her and at the dragon. He thought that if he was going to fall, he might as well try and take the dragon with him. He remembered Else saying, "Ansel the dragon killer." Perhaps she would get back to the village, or the town, or somewhere, and tell people what he had done. And he and the dragon would lie together in the heart of the glacier, and it would bear them slowly downhill towards the lowlands, and one day in a hundred years or more someone would find their bodies in the lake of melted ice at the glacier's snout and they would know that the tales of Ansel the dragon killer had been true.

It gave him comfort, of a chilly sort.

The dragon paused and watched him carefully, as if it suspected him of plotting something. But he knew that it couldn't resist him. Brock had been right: you needed live bait to trap a worm. It didn't have to be a girl, though. Anyone would do.

He flapped his arms at the dragon. He hooked his fingers into the sides of his mouth and pulled them wide and poked his tongue out. He started to dance, and only stopped when he felt another chunk of snow peel off and drop into the emptiness below. A small, sinister hole opened with a whispering sound between his feet. He looked down at it, and almost missed seeing the dragon as it ran at him.

It came fast, head down, wings folded, wary

of taking to the air with its broken tail. It covered the space between them faster than Ansel would have thought possible, and just before it reached him the snow beneath his feet gave way, and he and the dragon went down together.

18

Brock was not dead. He was stumbling through the blank white world the blizzard had left, keeping as much as he could to the lee of rocks where the snow came up only to his knees and not his hips. He had lost his sword. "Ansel!" he called, and "Else!"

As the last flurries of the blizzard had faded around them he had watched the dragon, and the dragon had watched him. It must have heard Else's screams, he thought, and been on its way towards them when the blizzard overtook it. Its ugly snout was white with crusted snow, and more snow had packed the grooves between its scales the way it packs sometimes between the stones of a wall. He looked into its yellow eyes and said as bravely as he could, "In the name of St Michael and St George. . ."

His voice trembled with cold and fear. The dragon, as usual, said nothing. It flapped its wings like a tent in a breeze. Groggily, Brock started to grope his way towards the same discovery that Ansel had made the day before. This wasn't the Devil's creature. It was just a creature.

It lunged without warning and he swung the sword as its long head arrowed towards him. The blade rang on scales hard as flint, and the shock jolted the sword's hilt from his frozen fingers. The dragon shrieked, drawing clumsily aside. He remembered how it had used its tail as a weapon at their first meeting, and guessed what was coming, but was too sluggish from the cold to avoid it. It hit him in the side of the head, a jarring blow that laid him in the snow. He tasted blood. He had bitten his tongue.

The dragon snorted angrily, but it did not

approach him. Perhaps the remains of his armour confused it and made it think he was not edible. Or perhaps it was afraid he'd sting again. Blood drizzled from a gash on its snout, showing suddenly scarlet as the clouds parted to let a thin wash of sunlight through. Brock's sword shone dazzlingly, planted upright in a snowdrift like Excalibur. The dragon flinched its head round to look. It went forward cautiously, shaking the snow from its claws at each step. It sniffed the sword. Then, tilting its head sideways, it took the blade between its teeth.

Brock watched it, too dazed to stand or even call out.

The dragon did not look at him again. It lifted the bright sword, opened its wings, and took clumsily to the sky. Its wingbeats raised a small new blizzard of powdery snow from the crests of the drifts as it soared over Brock and away.

After a while he managed to lift himself. The buffeting the beast had dealt him had left his neck stiff and his tongue swollen, but he had no other wounds. He thought of Else and Ansel, and felt suddenly ashamed of what he had done. Where were they? he wondered, looking around at the fresh whiteness of the snow. Had the dragon come upon them in the blizzard? Or were they hiding somewhere? Hiding from him now, as well as the beast, and he couldn't blame them for that. He cursed himself. He was supposed to be their protector. Small wonder that God had not granted him victory over the dragon. . .

There was no trace of their tracks in the new snow. He blundered across the mountain top calling out their names. "Else! Ansel! Forgive me!"

There was no reply, only the endless echoes bounding away over the snow and ringing back at him from the black rocks. And then, from over the hill's edge, the cry of the dragon.

He stopped, frozen there like an iron statue, listening. It came again, and then again, and mingled with it he thought he heard Else's shrill screaming.

He turned, trying to tell which was echo and which the true sound. It seemed to be coming from the other side of the ridge. He scrambled towards it, feeling with one hand for the knife in his belt, which was the only weapon he had left.

He pushed his way between snow-crusted rocks and stood at the top of the screes, looking down. Below him on the glacier a flake of colour showed, the only bright thing in the world. Else's dress. He went downhill towards it, slipping and stumbling, tumbling for long stretches, battering and buckling his armour and bruising the flesh beneath it. "Else!" he shouted. "It's me! Brock!"

Else looked up and saw him coming. She was not afraid. She was in too much pain to be afraid. When the dragon landed beside her she had thrown herself backwards and her ankle had caught in a fissure of the ice that lay beneath the snow and been wrenched round. Broken, she feared at first. A bad sprain at best. And she'd lain there and watched Ansel face the dragon, and the two of them fall down together into that black hole which opened under him in the snow, and she'd thought that there'd be no way down the mountain for her now. So she was not afraid of Brock. She raised herself up and watched as he came toiling towards her, a tiny figure growing slowly larger, shouting out every few minutes, "Else! Forgive me! I was wrong to use you so. My hatred for the dragon made me mad. You must believe me; I would never have let the creature harm you. . ."

Else decided to forgive him. If it were really only the two of them left alive upon that mountain then it would be foolish of her to hold a grudge.

"Where's Ansel?" Brock asked, when he drew nearer. "The dragon – have you seen the dragon?"

And Else just pointed at the chasm, to show him where the two of them had gone.

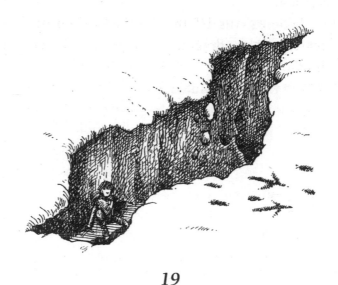

19

Ansel hit blue ice, hard enough to knock all the wind out of him. Hit blue ice and slithered, grabbing for handholds where no handholds were, pummelled by snow crashing down on him from above. He came to a stop twenty feet down, cradled in a crook of the ice, gawping up at the distant sky. Half of the snow ceiling had collapsed, letting daylight shaft down into the crevasse. The ice walls curved away from each other, filled with deep fissures and strange blue shadows. From overhangs trailed icicles taller than Ansel, and as he watched some of them fell, shattering with a sound like handbells.

He lifted his head cautiously, and looked for the dragon. It had fallen past him and lay in a deeper part of the crevasse, wedged tight, one sail-like wing stretched upwards so that it looked like the wreck of a small boat. It lay very still. *The fall has killed it*, he thought exultantly, and then immediately began to doubt, because it was so much bigger and fiercer and more alive than he was, and the fall had not killed *him*. He listened hard for a long time, but he could not hear it moving.

What he heard instead was a voice from up above him, calling his name.

"Ansel? Are you down there, boy?"

He looked up. Brock's head was poking over the ragged brim of the crevasse, looking down at him. "Thank Christ!" cried the dragon hunter, when he saw Ansel's face lift towards him. He turned his head and shouted to someone out of sight – Else, presumably – "He lives!" Then, looking back at Ansel, "I have the rope yet. We'll lower it. . ."

He vanished, and a smatter of dislodged snow

came down in Ansel's eyes. By the time he had wiped them Brock was back, paying out the rope. Ansel moved carefully, standing up on the treacherous ice and reaching up with both hands to touch the rope tip as it came jerking down. *When I touch it*, he thought, *I'll be as good as saved.*

But it was not to be that easy.

"First the worm," called Brock.

Ansel thought he'd heard wrong. The scalloped ice walls made strange echoes. Had they twisted the sense of Brock's words somehow? Surely his master could not mean—?

"The dragon," said Brock, very slowly and clearly. He pointed at the place where it lay. "You don't think I'll go back to that sneering landgrave without my trophy, do you? Not after the trouble I've been to. Get a rope around it, boy."

Ansel looked at the dragon. He sniffed, and smelled its animal smell, which had already begun to taint the cold, clean air. Whether it was alive or dead, he wanted nothing more to do with it. But Brock was his master, and Brock was the man on the end of the rope. He could no see choice for himself except to do as Brock asked.

He edged his slippery way down to it, hoping that it lay too deep for the rope to reach. But the rope was long. Brock shifted along the crevasse edge up above him and dangled it down just above the dragon. Ansel caught the end. The dragon's head was turned away from him, and he was glad of that. It was lying across two big hummocks of ice in such a way that it was quite easy for him to pass the end of the rope under it and around and under again and knot it tight.

"All right, boy," said Brock. "Now climb up. I'll need you up here to help me haul the beast up, won't I? Come on, Ansel; you can do it easily. Climb."

Ansel couldn't do it easily, but he managed. Numb hands clenching on the wet rope, he dragged himself up the sheer face of the ice, and when he was nearly at the top Brock and Else both reached over and caught him and heaved him over the edge, back into daylight. Afternoon sunlight lay on the snow. It was cold still, but it seemed warm to Ansel after the ice depths he had come from.

"And now for the dragon," Brock said.

They braced themselves against the rope, half afraid that the beast's dead weight would drag them down into the chasm along with it. But it came up easily: a weight to be sure, but not near as heavy as Ansel would have guessed. Hollow-boned, he thought. Like a big bird. A little straining, and it came up over the chasm's edge, tail first, wings flopping open like a Christmas goose.

It was only then, as it lay before them in the sunlight, that they saw that it was still alive. A faint, steady smoulder of hot breath came from its nostrils; its scaly chest rose and fell. Ansel, remembering how he had trussed it up, and how easily it might have woken and bitten his head off, turned away to be sick. Else, scrambling backwards on her bottom with her hurt leg dragging said almost angrily, "Kill it! Kill it! Kill it!"

Brock didn't need her advice. He drew his knife and stepped up to the dragon, wondering where best to strike – the throat? The heart? And then, slowly, the look of determination faded from his face and he lowered the knife again.

"Kill it, sir!" insisted Else.

"Not here," said Brock. Cutting a fathom from the rope's end, he wound it around the dragon's snout and knotted it tight. He cut another length and bound the beast's feet together, hobbling it. Else and Ansel stood and watched him.

He tightened the last knot and looked back at them triumphantly. "Not here. People might not believe it. If I take back its head men may say it's just the head of a corkindrille or some such. Such tricks have been known, I believe. No, I shall kill this dragon in the square of the town, with the landgrave and the bishop and all their people looking on."

"And how will you get it to town, sir?" Else said sullenly. "Expect us to drag it there, I suppose?"

"It's light," said Brock. "You felt how light it is. We'll build a sledge from pine branches. It's all downhill from here. We'll pull the animal behind us, over the snow. When we get lower you can run ahead and bring help from the village."

"I can't run anywhere," the girl said.

"Ansel, then."

And what if it wakes up while we're dragging it on this sledge? thought Ansel. *What if it wakes up and finds it doesn't much care for being dragged on sledges?* And he looked at Else and saw that she was thinking the same thing. But not Brock. Brock was walking around his prize, checking his knots and looking like a man who knew that God had been on his side all along.

20

When the peasants of Knochen saw Ansel coming down the steeps behind their village, they thought he was a ghost. And to be fair, he did look like one, ragged as he was, and wild-eyed, and with all those scrapes and bruises showing up the pallor of his face. Even when he drew near and they could see his shadow and hear the way the small stones rattled under his unghostly, stumbling feet, they still hung back from him. They'd not expected to see any of Brock's party again, not since the pack pony Brezel came clattering back alone down the mountain the day before, mad-eyed, bloody, frothed with sweat. They'd kept well away from that pony, most of them, sure that it would bring bad luck, and now they kept well away from Ansel. It seemed to them that the only way he could have survived on the dragon's hill was by selling his soul to Satan. And maybe he'd promised his new master *their* souls too. . .

It was Else's mother who broke their silence. Maybe she thought her luck couldn't get any worse. She was the one who'd taken care of Brezel, calming and combing him and bathing his wounds in salt water. Now she ran to Ansel. "Did you see my girl on the mountain?" she asked him as she reached out to grab him by both shoulders, gripping them tight to reassure herself that he was real. She touched his hands, his face, lifting his hair, staring at the grazes on his forehead. "Did you see my Else?"

Ansel stared back at her. He was a bit dazed to find himself the centre of so many people's attention. His world had narrowed to just Brock and Else and the dragon. He had forgotten there were so many others. He looked at Else's mother, and then realized what she had asked him.

He nodded.

And then she was hugging him, and all the villagers were round him, demanding to know if the dragon was dead, if the dragon hunter was victorious. All he could do was nod. He knew that if he let on that the beast still lived they would never come up the mountain and give the help that was needed.

"And Father Flegel?" someone asked.

He shook his head.

He had left Brock and Else resting at the snowline. The dragon lay trussed on the crude pine-branch sledge they had made for it. It had regained its senses sometime in the night, and they had been woken by its struggles and its muffled, threatening roars. But the ropes had held, and now it lay still, seemingly resigned, one evil yellow eye staring at the sky.

The villagers would not go near it at first. They crossed themselves or hid their faces, appalled at the thing Brock had brought back from the mountain with him. Brock had to threaten them before they'd help. "Here is the girl Else," he said, pointing her out where she stood reunited with her mother, the two of them holding to each other so tight and watching the other villagers as if daring them to try and prise them apart again. Brock said, "Here is the girl you would have given to this monster like a sacrifice upon a heathen altar. Shall I tell your landgrave how you treated her? Shall I tell your bishop how little faith you have in the goodness of God upon this mountain? Or shall you help me carry the beast to town, so that the whole world can see it vanquished?"

The villagers were silent. Brock scared them almost as much as the dragon. He was as ragged as the boy, and there was a look in his eyes that suggested his night on the mountain had made him into a madman or a saint – a man worth humouring, in either case. They still hung back, but when Else sat down on the dragon's tail and smirked at them first one and then another of the men edged forward, closer and closer to the monster, flinching backwards at every small sound and movement that it made. At last one drew close enough to jab its flank with the staff he carried. Another, not to be outdone, spat at it. "Why," said one, "it's just a big old lizard."

They brought more ropes and lashed it tighter, just to be sure. They cut fresh runners for the sledge, to replace the two rough logs that Ansel and Brock had used. They dragged it downhill to the track, where they were met by men bringing horses from the village. Behind the horses walked Brezel; clever Brezel, who had passed through that landslide somehow and found his own way back to Knochen. Brezel who knew better than to go near that dragon again and started snorting and whinnying and trying to turn away as soon as he got within twenty yards of it. Ansel had to run and take his halter to keep him from bolting. He stood stroking the pony's nose, watching the village men as they coaxed their horses closer to the beast.

It took a long while before they could be calmed enough to be hitched to the sledge traces, but at last they were attached and the strange procession set off towards the town. Ansel scrambled up on to Brezel's broad back, and Brezel farted like a trumpet. Else cast aside the branch she'd leaned on to limp down the mountain and rode on the sledge, sitting on the dragon. She was scared of it, but she hid her fear, enjoying the knowledge that her neighbours were now afraid of her. She did not even hop down from her perch when they came to fords and broken-down portions of the road, where the horses had to be unhitched and the villagers dragged sledge and dragon on by hand. Let them drag her too. That would show them!

Brock, missing his horse, walked beside the girl's mother. The woman seemed to have grown younger now that the weight of her grief was lifted from her. She still cried from time to time but they were sweet tears, like April rain. Brock was telling her the story of what had happened to them on the mountain, although it was not *quite* what had happened to them on the mountain, and the woman looked at him sideways as if she guessed that but didn't much mind. Now that he knew her daughter, Ansel could see how alike they were: she had the same wide mouth, the same habit of quirking her thick black eyebrows into a frown. She looked like Else grown up.

"What will you and your daughter do when the creature's killed?" Brock asked her. "You'll not be safe in Knochen. Once the dragon's dead and I'm gone away these brutes will kill you both to keep you silent."

Else's mother shrugged, and patted her bodice.

"I have a little money, sir. My husband's savings. I'll buy a cart in town and travel on. I'll be a tinker like my mother's people. Go far away from mountains, that's for sure."

And Ansel, hearing her, stroked Brezel's shaggy neck and thought, *Oh, me too! Never more any mountains for me!*

The procession grew bigger as they neared the town. People came from villages and farmsteads to see the thing on the sledge, and then joined in, children running alongside to pelt the trussed-up dragon with mud and pebbles, their fathers stepping up to help the exhausted burghers of Knochen whenever the sledge had to be coaxed over rough ground, or a gateway needed battering down to let it through. Reckless young men scrambled on the dragon's back to show off to their friends and flirt with Else. When a few had ventured up there and come down uneaten the mood grew festive. One man began to play the bagpipes, while another banged a drum. The dragon flinched at the strange new noises. It tried to roar, but it was gagged too tightly to make a sound. Ansel thought he knew how it felt. Watching the flies that clustered thickly about its eyes he felt a sudden, guilty pity for it. But only for a moment. The parade was swelling quickly as the burghers of the town came running out to see what Brock had brought them.

They were silent at first when they realized what it was. Then, slowly, the excitement spread. It sounded like a wind coming, rushing over the treetops in a wood. And Ansel found himself being kissed, patted, lifted off Brezel's back to ride with Brock upon the shoulders of the crowd, in through the town gates and up the hill to the cathedral square.

21

They built a pen for the dragon there. The
carpenters who had been hired to make wooden
scaffolding for the masons at work on the
cathedral took their tools and stocks of wood and
made a cage instead: four barred walls and a
barred roof, just large enough to hold the beast,
anchored with ropes to heavy stones which they
dragged from the building site. It was almost dark
by that time. Torches and braziers were set up

around the cage, casting crazy shadows across the cobbles.

Brock reached in through the bars and cut the ropes which bound the dragon's legs and wings. It scrambled upright, claws scraping on the strange-feeling stones beneath it. It looked smaller than it had on the mountain, and it was certainly shabbier; stained with mud and spittle, with patches of bare and bird-pale flesh showing through where the ropes had rubbed its scales off. Its yellow eyes stared round at the crowd. They jeered at it, and laughed when someone threw a rotten cabbage which hit it between the eyes and made it flinch. Then Brock took a halberd from one of the town's guards and managed after a long struggle to cut some of the ropes which held its mouth closed. It snapped the rest itself and slammed its wounded muzzle against the bars. Its dreadful roar bellowed across the square, crashing from the walls of the cathedral and the landgrave's palace. The crowd scurried backwards, leaving Brock to stand alone beside the cage. When they saw that the carpenters' work was sound and the beast could not get free they started to edge in again, but each time it moved or made a sound they fell back, all of them at once, like a ripple in water.

Brock looked round at them, pleased at the impression that his catch had made. He ran his eyes over the ring of watching faces: children and ancients, peasants and paupers, mendicants, merchants, mountebanks, soldiers and priests, plain women and pretty ones. As far as he could tell the whole town had turned out to watch him kill the beast. The landgrave's secretary was at the front of the crowd making drawings of it, frowning each time they jostled him, with a boy at his side to hold his inkhorn and spare pens.

"So where is His Lordship?" asked Brock, in an actorly voice which he meant the whole square to hear. "The landgrave should be here to see me dispatch the beast."

The secretary looked up from his drawing. He wore spectacles of wood and glass, the first ever seen in that region. There was a smear of ink on the side of his nose. "The landgrave is away at present, sir. The emperor is hunting in the forest, and the landgrave has gone to pay his respects and join the sport."

"Sport?" Brock did his best to hide his disappointment. "I wonder what sport he will find in the emperor's woods. Boar? Deer? A badger or two?

There was better hunting on his own mountain all along."

The crowd cheered. Brock looked thoughtful. It seemed a shame that he had dragged the beast all this way if the lord of the place was not present to watch him kill it. "How far to these woods?" he asked.

"A half day's ride," the secretary said.

"Then send a messenger to fetch him home. Tell him to bring the emperor if he wishes. Tell him there is sport to be had here in his own town; if he hurries, he can be present when I slay this wild savage heathen monster. But he must hurry, for I do not think we can keep it penned up for long."

He looked at the wild savage heathen monster, hoping that it would add some drama to his words by roaring, or barging the bars of its cage. But the dragon seemed to have given up; its big head hung down, and apart from a quick trembling in the muscles of its haunches it might as well have been a carven statue.

That night they gave Ansel a bed of his own to sleep in, in a room of his own, next to Brock's, in the town's best inn. It felt strange to be lying on a soft straw mattress again after his time on the mountain. He blew out the candle and watched the wavery orange light of the fires in the square ripple around the edges of the shutters. Songs were being sung down there, and dances danced, and beer drunk, while abuse and rubbish was hurled at the captive dragon. They were slinging hunks of old meat into its cage, and saying "Oooh!" and "Aaah!" as it sullenly tore them up and wolfed them down. Ansel wondered if Else and her mother were down there. He had not seen them since the dragon was carried in through the gates, and he could not be sure that they had come into the town at all. It felt strange to think that he might not see Else again, or have his chance to bid her farewell, after the dangers that they'd come through together.

He slept, and dreamed that this was all a dream and that he was still on the mountain. The dragon hunted him, howling.

When he woke it was quiet. No sound from the square, only the soft light of the dying-down fires lapping at the shutters' rims. Ansel's stomach ached from all the rich food he had crammed into it the night before.

He knew he could not sleep again, for fear of falling back into the same dream. He rose and went downstairs instead, stepping carefully over the potboys sprawled in the inn's big lower room, lifting the latch and letting himself out into the chill night. The moon was low, resting on the shoulder of the Drachenberg. The town was quiet. Even the revellers in the square had grown bored of taunting the captive dragon and gone to their beds. Ansel walked past the snoozing guards who huddled around braziers of dull red coals and went up to the dragon's cage.

It was not asleep. He saw the moon-gleam on its eye as he came close to it. He saw its scars and wounds in the moonlight. *Poor dragon*, he thought. *The last of its kind, maybe.* It seemed wrong that it should end up here, penned and mocked. It was not evil that had made it eat men and sheep and horses, any more than evil made a fox kill chickens. It was an animal; that was all.

The dragon snorted, and the hot cloud of its breath drifted past Ansel like stinking smoke. It pushed its head against the cage and there was a creaking sound; a wrenching. He looked down and saw where the ropes which held the cage door shut were fraying. All night long it must have been nudging against the bars with that same patient motion, too gentle to be noticed by the guards or the townspeople who came to gawp at it. And now the ropes were almost worn through. Ansel stood and watched. He knew that he should warn someone, but he didn't. He just stood there, and strand by strand by the rope frayed through.

The dragon, perhaps recognizing his scent out of all the baffling scents of the town, gave a low growl and barged at the bars. The ropes strained. One snapped. The dragon shoved its nose out through the gap between the door and cage, then drew it back and barged again. The remaining ropes gave way and the door swung wide.

Ansel kept walking carefully backwards while the dragon eased itself cautiously out into the square. It flexed its long neck and stretched its wings and he felt again the cold terror that he had known on the mountain. He had grown so used to that feeling that he almost welcomed it.

"Hey!" shouted a man's voice behind him. "Hey! The beast's free!"

There were cries of alarm; curses; scuffling sounds as the guards snatched up their spears and halberds. Running footsteps, as some men fled. Others came past Ansel towards the dragon, their weapons held out nervously in front of them. One man shook Ansel and shouted angrily in his face, wanting to know why he hadn't warned them that the monster was loose.

Even if Ansel had had a voice, he would not have been able to answer. How could he explain that he pitied the dragon, and half wanted it to be free again?

Another man said, "Leave him. It's the dragon hunter's boy; he's dumb."

The dragon roared. The guard serjeant, braver than his men, lurched forward, jabbing his halberd at it. It snatched the weapon in its jaws and bit the shaft in half. The rusty blade rang as it dropped on the cobbles, and like an echo came the clattering of other weapons being thrown down as the men took flight. In one of the houses across the square a woman screamed. The dragon swung its head this way and that, scenting prey everywhere, confused by the sounds of panic which came from every doorway and street opening in the straggle of buildings which faced the cathedral. Stalking towards the closest house it shoved its head in through a shuttered window, groping inside in just the same way that it groped inside the shepherd's shelter on the mountain on the morning when Ansel first saw it. Shrieks and shouts came from inside the house, and the crying of a scared child.

Ansel found himself moving towards it. He looked down and saw his own feet moving him across the moonlit cobbles without his thinking about it. He knew he had to stop the dragon. Brock was still abed most likely: they'd have trouble waking him after all the wine which Ansel had seen him drink. Anyway, it was not Brock's fault that the thing was free.

Ansel flapped his hands at the dragon, but it had its tail to him, its head deep in the stricken house, whose walls were beginning to show cracks as the beast forced more and more of itself in through the window. Ansel picked up a cobble that its claws had gouged loose as it crossed the square and threw it as hard as he could, but the dragon only twitched, then ignored him and went on trying to stuff itself into that house.

Helpless, he felt his face crumple up as if he were a little boy again, getting ready to wail in anger or unhappiness. He hated the dragon. He hated the mountain. He hated the town. He hated the life that had led him here, Brock and his father and all of it. He hated being alone. He wanted Else with him again. He wanted his mother. And he felt all that hatred and want starting to gather somewhere behind his breastbone, a knot of pressure which grew and grew until he couldn't breathe, or swallow, or think, until he was sure he was going to explode.

The house door burst open. A terrified family spilled out into the square in their nightclothes, the older children carrying the younger ones, their mother and father lugging an aged grandfather between them in a high-backed chair.

The dragon, scenting them, tugged its head free of their crumbling house front and wheeled towards them. And Ansel ran towards it with that impossible knot inside him, and let it blare out of his mouth in a shout. He spewed sound. It was as if he had saved up the breath of every word he might have uttered in all his years of speechlessness and let them all out at once. He roared at the dragon, loud enough to make it forget the huddled family in front of it and remember him. Loud enough to make the whole square clang like a swung bell.

"No!"

In the quiet afterwards, as he gasped in a great breath of air, he saw Else and her mother watching him from the end of one of the streets which opened off the square. They looked as astonished as he was by the noise he'd made. Catching his breath, he started to smile at them, and then he heard the dragon's flinty claws go click, click, click upon the cobbles as it began to run at him.

He turned and took off running himself, heading nowhere, seeing the cathedral loom up in front of him like a cliff. At its foot was a cave; an unfinished doorway screened with sackcloth and tarred canvas. He could hear the dragon's talons scraping across the cobbles behind him. Then they stopped, and he looked back half-hoping it had given up, but it had simply taken to the air, wings spread, half leaping and half soaring across the empty square in its pursuit of him.

He reached the doorway, crashed against the sackcloth screen, found a gap in it, and shot into the cathedral like a rabbit down its burrow.

For a moment he was alone in the cool and sacred shadows with only the slap of his running feet for company. Then the screens on the doorway behind him ripped and the dragon was inside with him, its snorting breath echoing under the high vaultings of the roof. Light came in with it – a dropped lamp in the house it had been menacing had started a fire –

and its ungainly shadow spread across the newly paved floor as it stretched out its neck and its big head swung to and fro, snuffing for Ansel.

He kept running, through ranks of pillars which rose around him like trees in a stone forest. He was looking for another door, but the cathedral seemed to be turning around him in the dark and he could not see one. At the end of the nave a spidery tower of scaffolding rose, marking the place where the masons were at work on the spire. In the midst of it, as if in a tall cage, a ladder stretched upwards, like Jacob's, into Heaven. Ansel flung himself at it and went up, up, feeling the dragon's jaws close on the lower rungs and yank it furiously aside just as he reached a planked platform at the top. He heard the ladder go crashing down behind him as he crossed the platform and started to climb a second.

He was halfway up it when he heard the sound he had been fearing: the whoosh and crack of the dragon's wings. It had learned to fly again, despite the injury he'd done its tail. He climbed faster, and the scaffolding tower shook as the dragon crashed against it, clinging to the struts with the claws of its feet and wings, shoving its hungry, angry head in through the gaps between them. Its roar rolled through the cathedral. The scaffolding swayed, wood grinding against the stone of the new walls.

Above him now there was light. Wooden hoardings screened the spire's unfinished top, but there were gaps, and through one of these he saw the moonlight shine. He scrambled over the ladder's top on to another platform and hurled himself at the opening.

Out in the open again, he fell, and landed hard on a stone ledge, where carved gargoyles looked out across the town towards the dragon's mountain. Below him – a terrifyingly long way below – smoke was ghosting above the rooftops, and the streets were full of confused flocks of townspeople, some fleeing the dragon while others tried to fight the spreading fire.

He listened, ignoring the noises from below, and heard the dragon's claws go by a few inches from him as it climbed up the inside of the spire. The wooden hoarding lurched, and workmen's tools and fresh-cut stones went avalanching down over the roofs and buttresses into the square. It lurched a second time, then the planking gave way and the dragon writhed itself out through the wreckage like some enormous hatchling freeing itself from a wooden egg.

It crouched on the spire's unfinished top,

silhouetted against the sinking moon, like the king of all the gargoyles. It did not seem to see Ansel. Perhaps the smells of burning from below disguised his scent. Perhaps it had forgotten him. It was staring towards the black bulk of its mountain.

*

In his room at the inn Brock found himself being shaken awake. Found himself being pummelled and slapped and treated in ways that no hero deserved. He groaned, half rising, regretting all the cups of wine he'd emptied, which had bred a hard ache in his head and made the inn's floor tip like a ship in steep seas.

"It's loose!" someone shouted, right in his face, and by the gathering glow from his window he saw that it was Else.

"What – sun coming up already?" he asked mildly, squinting at the window, where the girl's mother stood, having just flung wide the shutters. Outside there was some shouting and screaming going on, and people running.

Else slapped him again. "Your dragon's got loose, and it's eating people and shoving houses down and what are you going to do about it?"

"It has set the whole town blazing with its fiery breath," said her mother.

"Loose. . ." mumbled Brock, beginning to understand. But by then Else and her mother and half a dozen other people of the town were round him, buckling him into his armour, pressing a sword into his hand. He lost sight of Else as they manhandled him downstairs and out into the smoky, screamy night, but some of the braver townsfolk went behind him to the square to watch him slay the monster.

From high above Ansel saw him step out into the open space between the cathedral and the landgrave's palace. His armour swirled with reflected flames. His face showed pale as he looked up to where the townspeople pointed. "Worm!" he shouted nervously. "Come down and face me!"

The dragon heard and looked down at him. A tremor ran through its body. It half opened its wings. Shifting its perch on the spire it dislodged a gargoyle, and Brock had to jump aside as the stone figure shattered in front of him.

Don't heed him, dragon, thought Ansel, hiding there in the sky. *Don't fly down there. He'll kill you this time, or you'll kill him, and then the townspeople will kill you.*

The dragon watched Brock. Its maimed tail

flexed, rasping over the spire's stones. Low in its throat it made a gurgling growl.

Go home, thought Ansel. Because it belonged on its mountain, and he wished that it would just fly away there, and live quietly, up high somewhere, keeping out of the way of people now that it knew what trouble people were, and maybe some day finding another of its kind. . .

It shrieked suddenly, drowning all his thoughts, driving everything but fear out of his head. It spread its wings and pitched forward, launching itself clear of the spire and dropping into the square. Ansel heard the wind rushing through its tattered flight feathers as it went. Below him, Brock saw it coming and made ready, knowing he must not fail this time, with all these people watching. He gripped his sword and set his feet well apart and tried not to cringe as the dragon's cry filled the square.

It dropped till it was almost upon him, and then, with a twitch of its wings, it saved itself and soared upward, over the upturned faces of the watchers crammed in the narrow street behind Brock, over the roofs of the burning buildings. Its wounded tail swiped down a chimney pot from the landgrave's palace. It circled the cathedral tower and Ansel looked down on it and saw the fire shining upwards through its spread wings, showing him every bone and quill of them, like sunshine streaming through two leaves.

It gave one last cry, then flew away. The town's walls could not keep it in. It went like a dark, ungainly bird, low over the farmlands and the woods, and Ansel lost it for a while against the shadows of the land, and then saw it one last time, far off, black as a bat against a patch of moonlight on the distant snows.

When the landgrave rode back into the town late the next morning he found no dragon waiting for him, just three streets burned down to ash and rubble, the palace roof and the tower of the new cathedral damaged and his people more fearful and superstitious than ever. This did not please him. The emperor's own envoy and half the young men of the imperial court had ridden with him to see the strange beast which Brock had brought down from the mountain. He felt like a fool for believing the message which had drawn him home.

"But it *was* a dragon," his secretary said, showing him a handful of feathers, a few scales, and a scratchy, hesitant drawing of something that looked like a toothy chicken.

The landgrave held his drawing up in the light from a window and frowned. "Johannes Brock has made fools of you all," he declared. "What he brought down from the Drachenberg was nothing but a big bird. An eagle, no doubt, with some of its feathers shaved off." He flung the picture aside and gnawed at his fingers as he tried to think how he could apologize to his important guests. "Where *is* Johannes Brock anyway?" he asked darkly.

But when his servants went to look for the dragon hunter, there was not a trace of him to be found.

Nothing more was ever seen of the Drachenberg Worm. The scales and feathers were kept, along with the drawings. Some centuries later a descendant of the landgrave found them in his Cabinet of Curiosities, and showed them to a natural philosopher, a pupil of the great Linnaeus, who studied them for a while and then concluded that the whole thing was a medieval hoax. Those moth-eaten feathers proved nothing, he said, while the scales had perhaps been taken from a pangolin. As for the drawings, they were as crude as one would expect from such a brutish era, and portrayed a most unlikely creature, part reptile and part bird. He was far more intrigued by the remains of a skull discovered beside a river on the Drachenberg, which seemed to prove that *crocodiles* had once lived upon the mountain. . .

22

Ansel, like his master, guessed there'd be no welcome any more in that town for dragon hunters. He remembered that guard who had shaken and shouted at him in the square. For all he knew the whole town blamed him for letting the dragon out of its cage.

He scrabbled back inside the spire and down into the nave again, climbing down the scaffolding itself for the last few fathoms, where the dragon had knocked away the ladder. Outside, the town was still burning merrily. Brezel was in the stable behind the inn, tethered and kicking at his stall while flags of burning thatch eddied across the yard. Ansel untied him and rode out of the stable with his head down in case the townspeople saw him, but he need not have worried; they were all too busy running about shouting and trying to organize chains of buckets to douse the blaze.

There were no guards at the town gate. The boy and the pony slipped out unnoticed into dark and silent countryside. There Ansel found a hollow under a stand of birch trees, and lay down and slept.

The dragon got into his dreams again, as he knew it always would. It was as if it had not flown away at all, just made itself small and crept inside his head.

By the time he woke again the sun was already high in the sky. Brezel was cropping the grass a little way off. Ansel scrambled to the top of his dell and lay on his stomach and looked back at the town. A thin haze of smoke still hung above it, but the fires were out. He wondered if he should go back and look for Brock. He wondered if he should go south, back to his father's inn. And as he lay there wondering, he saw a little wagon come out through the town gates and start along the lakeside road towards him. Brezel stopped eating and raised his head, and his ears went up inquiringly. A tiny, shabby painted wagon it was, drawn by two horses. As it came closer Ansel too could hear it jingling. Strings of small bells hung from its roof, sparkling and clanking in the sunlight. It was a tinker's cart, he guessed, selling knives and needles from town to town.

He saw no reason to hide himself from tinkers, so he came out of the hollow under the birches and went closer to the road to watch it pass. He was surprised when the driver reined the horses in and sat looking at him. He wondered if he was in trouble, and was getting ready to run when a girl climbed out of the cart and came limping across the grass towards him.

It was Else. Who else but Else? The driver was her mother. So they had bought their cart and they were leaving.

"Ansel!" said Else. "We heard the dragon ate you!"

She took him by his hand and led him down to the road where the cart waited. Brezel ambled after them, flicking his tail to whisk away the flies which were waking in the spring sunshine. The horses turned their long heads to stare at him, and Else's mother nodded at Ansel and smiled her shy smile.

"We're bound for the lowlands," Else said. "We'll buy things and sell them, in the towns we pass. You want to come?"

Ansel wondered what to do. He looked back at the town again.

"Don't worry about him," said Else, guessing that he was thinking about Brock. "He left in the night, not long after the dragon. He's safe."

How does she know? thought Ansel. He looked at the wagon again. It was old and shabby, and Else and her mother did not seem to have any goods to sell, only a bundle of blankets. Then the blankets lifted, and Brock's face grinned out from under them.

"Come on, Ansel," the dragon hunter said. "You can't stay in this town. They are ill-tempered, unforgiving people. Do you know, they blamed *me* for setting loose the dragon? Said I was in league with it, and had plotted with it to destroy their new church? I believe they might have burned me for a witch if Else and her good mother hadn't taken pity on me. . ."

He sat up, shedding the blankets. He had taken

off his armour and he was wearing the old stained tunic that he'd worn when he and Ansel rode north together. "I don't know where we're bound," he said. "Warm countries, without mountains, for a start. And after that, perhaps Carpathia. I've heard the peasants there live in terror of make-believe beings called *vampyrs*, who drink blood and shun the daylight. And the best part is, they are said to crumble into a mere handful of ashes when you kill them. Ashes are easier to come by than corkindrilles' skulls. And you do not even need armour, or a sword; apparently some wreaths of garlic and a pointy stick suffice. We could set up as vampyr slayers. . ."

Else's mother laughed wearily from the front of the cart. Else said, "Don't mind him, Ansel. But you're welcome to come with us. If you want to."

Ansel just stood there. He wasn't used to deciding what his life should be. There had always been someone to tell him what he must do before, but Else wasn't telling him, she was only asking. She looked at him, and after a while she shrugged and turned away and limped back around the cart. Ansel watched her climb back on to the seat beside her mother. He watched her mother gather up the reins, and the horses shake themselves and start to walk. The wagon rolled off slowly, bells jingle-jangling, Brock looking back at Ansel from under the canopy.

Ansel remembered the roar that had come out of him the night before. He had grown so used to being silent that he had not tried to speak since; he wasn't sure that there were any sounds left in him. But he opened his mouth and there were the words, waiting inside him to be spoken, his gift from the dragon, better than gold. He spoke them. He *shouted* them. He scrambled on to Brezel's back and grabbed two handfuls of mane and smacked his heels against the pony's flanks and kept on shouting as he cantered after the cart. It was good to shout, and to feel the big sounds pouring out of his throat. He shouted to urge Brezel on, and to make Else's mother stop. He shouted the way all boys shout, the same way the birds were singing in the blackthorn trees, for sheerest joy.

"Wait! Wait! WAIT FOR ME!"

ACKNOWLEDGEMENTS

With thanks to my editors at Scholastic,
Marion Lloyd and Alice Swan.

Discover the brilliant world of

MORTAL ENGINES

Philip Reeve's futuristic fantasy series

MORTAL ENGINES
PREDATOR'S GOLD
INFERNAL DEVICES
A DARKLING PLAIN

A world where moving cities hunt each other down

Mortal Engines

Infernal Devices

A WEB OF AIR

PHILIP REEVE

The sixth superb story in the

MORTAL ENGINES

series is coming soon.

The clever young engineer, Fever Crumb, is swept up in a race to build a flying machine. Her mysterious companion is a boy who talks to angels. Powerful enemies will kill to possess their new technology - or to destroy it.

A WEB OF AIR is the thrilling sequel to FEVER CRUMB, the story set centuries before MORTAL ENGINES that tells how great cities began to build giant engines to make their first predatory journeys across the wastelands.

Publishing in April 2010.

Don't miss it!